T0286749

More Critical Praise for K'wan

for *The Reluctant King*

"K'wan is exceptionally gifted at ratcheting up suspense ... There's no denying the writer's talent for dark, gritty fiction. It's a page-turner."
—*Kirkus Reviews*

"Just when you think you know how this story is going to end, K'wan hits you with one his infamous curveballs that will stop you in your tracks. *The Reluctant King* by K'wan is an enjoyable start to this new series and will make you anticipate the second installment."
—*Urban Reviews*

"New York city council member Chancellor King and his socialite wife are regarded as modern-day royalty, but King's ambition to rise in the political world is threatened by an unambitious son and some dark family secrets."
—*Publishers Weekly*

for *Black Lotus*

- Selected for the Library Services for Youth in Custody 2015 In the Margins Book Award List
- One of *Library Journal*'s Best African American Fiction Books of 2014

"[A] heart-thumping thriller . . . K'wan does a masterful job of keeping readers on their toes right up to the very last page."
—*Publishers Weekly*

"Fans expecting another thug-in-the-street story will be pleasantly surprised at this rough police procedural."
—*Library Journal*

"Yet another heart-thumping thriller by this hip-hop author who delivers."
—Library Services for Youth in Custody

"This book features the sublime story and character development that K'wan is known for."   —*Urban Reviews*

for *Black Lotus 2: The Vow*

• Nominated for the 2021 Street Lit Writer of the Year Award

"*Black Lotus 2: The Vow* is full of the cinematic action and drama that K'wan is known for. Readers will be anxiously waiting for the next installment."   —*Urban Reviews*

"K'wan delivers a lean, tightly plotted tale that balances noir aesthetics with comic book flair. Fans of pulp and urban lit will be well satisfied."   —*Publishers Weekly*

"[A] riveting read from start to finish . . . Excellent."
                                 —*Exclusive Magazine*

"From page one to the last, *Black Lotus 2: The Vow* is a high-wire act with no net. A smart refiguring of hard-boiled with a nitro injection of new-age sensibilities."
        —Reed Farrel Coleman, author of *Walking the Perfect Square*

"Like a cool, hip, and fun evening at a vintage drive-in, *Black Lotus 2: The Vow* takes me back to a time when Jim Kelly, Pam Grier, and Fred Williamson graced the big screen. Throw in some Bruce Lee and a little *The Last Dragon* and you have a hell of a butt-kicking, action-filled ride."   —Ace Atkins, author of *The Shameless*

"*Black Lotus 2: The Vow* is a thrilling roller-coaster ride of a mystery that kept me on the edge of my seat!"
        —Bernice L. McFadden, author of *The Book of Harlan*

FALSE IDOLS

A RELUCTANT KING NOVEL

FALSE IDOLS

BOOK 2: THE BOOK OF THIEVES

K'WAN

BROOKLYN, NEW YORK

Published by Akashic Books
©2024 K'wan

Paperback ISBN: 978-1-63614-177-0
Hardcover ISBN: 978-1-63614-176-3

Library of Congress Control Number: 2023949405

Akashic Books
Brooklyn, New York
Instagram, X, Facebook: AkashicBooks
info@akashicbooks.com
www.akashicbooks.com

For Tabby

THE KING FAMILY

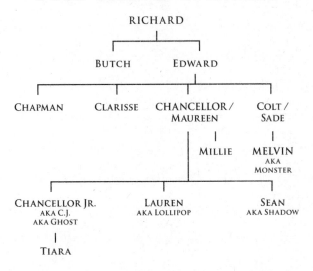

RICHARD

BUTCH — EDWARD

CHAPMAN — CLARISSE — CHANCELLOR / MAUREEN — COLT / SADE

MILLIE — MELVIN
AKA
MONSTER

CHANCELLOR JR. — LAUREN — SEAN
AKA C.J. AKA LOLLIPOP AKA SHADOW
AKA GHOST

TIARA

THE MONARCHY

KING

CHAPMAN KING

COUNCIL OF LORDS

HENRY — LITO — CARMINE — ROCCO — BILLY
ATUME — GARCIA — LUPENZA — SALVATORE — WONG

PROLOGUE

"I still can't believe you got me up in this spot like this," Shay said, clicking her gum. She was a slender brown-skinned girl with perky tits and long legs. She wore her hair in finger waves, streaked with blond. They were on the third floor of a tenement building somewhere in the Bronx. Piss stained the floor and they had to step over a junkie who was passed out on the stairs to reach the landing.

"I told you to wait in the car," said Anthony, a short dude with a thick beard and potbelly. A Mets hat was pulled low over his sneaky eyes.

"And you'd have taken even longer if I'd let you come up here alone," Shay responded. "You know how y'all niggas get to smoking weed and talking shit. You'd have taken forever and I ain't trying to miss my movie. So I'm babysitting your ass. I don't see why this couldn't wait until after the movie."

"Because business always comes before pleasure. Won't take me but a minute to grab this money. I gotta drop it off on the way to the theater, so we ain't gonna miss your stupid movie." Anthony was tired of Shay's bitching, and had she not promised to give him a blow job in the theater, he wouldn't have even bothered. Shay had a shot of head that was out of this world, and he wasn't about to pass it up.

Anthony knocked on the dented brown apartment door and waited. A few seconds later, he heard heavy footfalls approaching, then the peephole jiggled. After several locks were undone, the door opened and Anthony found himself confronted by the apartment's tenant, Delores. At one time Delores had been a knockout—tall, redbone, with natural hair that hung down her back. But the thing glaring at Anthony with suspicious eyes was a shadow of that. Delores was now so thin she looked emaciated, her skin bruised and pocked. Her long, luxurious hair was withered and falling out in spots. Track marks lined her arms, one still wet with blood. Whatever Delores had been, she would never be again.

"'Sup, D?" Anthony greeted, and invited himself into the apartment.

Shay timidly made to follow, but the haggard woman blocked her path.

"Who this bitch?" Delores looked Shay up and down. "Anthony, you know the rule about bringing new faces around here."

"She ain't nobody. Stop acting like that, Delores. Let her pass."

Delores lingered a few seconds before finally stepping aside.

Shay followed Anthony into the living room where two young men sat on a couch playing video games. At a cluttered dining room table sat another man, slightly older, packaging drugs. There was more heroin on the table than Shay had ever seen. She knew Anthony hustled, but up to this point she'd had no idea how deep in the game he was. She made a note to herself to start taxing his ass double whenever he wanted some pussy.

"'Sup wit' it, Vic?" Anthony said to the man packaging the drugs. "Y'all got that ready for me?"

"Fo' sho'." Vic nodded at one of the young dudes playing video games.

The kid put his controller down and disappeared into one of the bedrooms. A few seconds later he returned, carrying a plastic shopping bag, which he handed to Anthony.

Anthony held the bag at arm's length. "Y'all can't pack cash no better than this?"

"What you wanted us to do," Vic said, "go to the bank and ask for envelopes for all our drug money?"

"Do I need to count this?"

"You know I wouldn't play with Christian's money," Vic said. "It's all there."

"Anybody seen Lord Liberace today?" Anthony asked. That was what he called Christian behind his back, because of his eccentric way of dressing.

"Better be careful how you talk about that one there," Delores said. "You know the devil got ears everywhere."

"Shut your scary ass up, D." Anthony chuckled. "He just a nigga out here getting a dollar like the rest of us, but you act like he's Count Dracula."

"One blood sucker is as good as the next," Delores mumbled, then dropped down onto the couch to get her works together. As she started to tie off her arm, there was a knock at the door. She looked around at the men in the room, but none of them seemed interested in answering it. "Lazy muthafuckas." She got up and shambled toward the door, throwing Shay a dirty look. "I keep telling you about having all this traffic in and out of my house!" Delores pressed her eye to the peephole. At first, she didn't see anything but darkness. Then came a blinding light.

* * *

Shay had been standing against the wall near the entrance to the living room. She didn't like the way the boys playing the video games were looking at her, so she'd removed herself from their line of vision. She tapped her foot impatiently, wishing that Anthony would hurry up and finish his business. When Delores passed her on the way to the front door, she got a whiff of the woman, who smelled like she hadn't washed her ass in a week. It was definitely time to go and Shay was about to tell Anthony as much when she heard what sounded like a small explosion. Her eyes cut down the hall in time to see Delores's brains leap from her head and paint the wall.

The door shook once . . . twice . . . then burst open. Several men flooded the apartment, all holding guns with murder in their eyes. Trailing them was one of the largest, ugliest men Shay had ever laid eyes on, also armed. He had dark eyes that were slightly off-center, and a flat nose like a boxer who had been punched one time too many. Battle scars marked his face, and his big black lips were dry like he used sandpaper for Chapstick. This man was truly hard to look at, but his most disturbing feature was his large, misshapen head. It reminded Shay of a jack-o'-lantern they'd decorated in school back in the day; Halloween had fallen on a Friday that year, so the pumpkin sat out in the classroom all weekend; when the kids came back to school on Monday, it had begun to rot and was collapsing on one side.

The beast approached with slow, menacing steps. Shay backed up against the wall and thought she was about piss herself, when he placed one of his thick, dry fingers under her chin and forced her to look into his eyes. Those cold, dead eyes. His lips parted into a wicked grin, showing off a mouthful of yellowing teeth. When he spoke, his breath was so rancid that she threw up a little in her mouth.

"I wonder if you taste as good as you look," the man said in a voice that sounded like a car's motor.

"I . . . I . . ."

"Don't flatter yourself, bitch. You ain't got enough meat on your bones for me. Get in there with the rest of them." He shoved her into the living room.

The other armed men already had the living room on lockdown. Anthony, Vic, and the others sat wearing looks ranging from shock to fright. The beast pushed Shay onto the couch, and she landed between the two boys who had been playing video games. They all looked too terrified to speak, but Anthony eventually found his voice.

"Yo, Monster, what the fuck is this?"

"This is me, coming to give you a royal decree. Your little establishment here falls outside the boundaries set by the Monarchy. And by order of the king of Five Points, all rogue operations are to be shut down immediately. Traitors to the crown will be dealt with." It sounded like Monster had been rehearsing these words all day.

"Big homie, what you talking about?" Vic spoke up. "We ain't betrayed no crown. This is all Christian's shit we moving. Same arrangement we been having in place since I came on board. What's this new shit?" The system started at the top of the food chain: Ghost hitting Christian with product, which Christian would in turn distribute to dudes like Vic to move on the streets. As far as Vic knew, that hadn't changed with the new pecking order.

"New king, new rules," Monster said to Anthony with a shrug. "The problem we have here is that your boss feels like he's exempt from the program. He got the memo, same as the rest of the generals who served under Ghost, but I guess he don't read so good. He thinks he's bigger than the Monarchy, and I now find myself in the uncomfortable position of needing to remind him of how small he really is."

Monster raised his pistol and shot Vic in the head, then turned back to Anthony, who looked like he was about to pass out.

"Monster . . . you know me, man. How far we go back?"

"Far enough to know that you'll make sure my message is delivered. Tell the so-called Prince of the Night that I'll be seeing him, and when I do, he'll either kneel before the throne or bleed on it."

PART I

THE LONG FALL

CHAPTER 1

The afternoon sky was overcast, a heavy shade of gray broken up by occasional patches of blue. It had been threatening to rain all day, but every time the clouds swelled and threatened to belch water over the city, the sun would peek back out.

Shadow was out and about enjoying his latest toy, a matte-black Mercedes-Benz G-Class SUV. It had been an early graduation gift from his parents and Shadow loved it more than anything. He'd owned it for only a few weeks and had already nailed three broads in the backseat. His mom had gotten on him about taking it to the car wash every few days, but he played it off as being so appreciative of the vehicle, rather than admitting that he needed to clean the scent of his various sex partners from the interior.

Shadow loved to fuck. So much, in fact, that his friends often joked that he loved pussy more than money. This is what had him creeping out of New Jersey that afternoon. Her name was Gina, if Shadow recalled correctly. He had only known her for a few hours before talking her out of her panties. Shadow had met her that morning at the gun range in Union, New

Jersey. The rules at ranges were more lax out there than the spots he knew about in New York. In Jersey, all you needed was to be over eighteen with a valid ID. He had been getting some practice in with a sweet Glock 19 that he'd seen his homie Pain handling recently on the block. Pain was always tapped into the latest weapons of mass destruction. He had even shown Shadow a rocket launcher once, though it was the Glock that really caught Shadow's eye.

Shadow had been fucking around with the Glock in one stall, while Gina and a friend were shooting in the next. He had watched as Gina handled an AK. The gun was almost taller than she was, and Shadow had been expecting to get a good laugh at watching her try to fire it, but to his surprise, Gina handled the assault rifle with ease. This clearly wasn't her first time firing one.

Shadow had caught up with her as she and her friend were leaving. He made a bit of small talk, and forty minutes later he found himself liquored up and engaged in a threesome at Gina's apartment in Jersey City. Gina and her girl proved to be real freaks. This might have been due in part to the ecstasy they had popped, courtesy of Shadow. He didn't indulge very often, but always kept a few pills on him for just such occasions.

When the girls had finished with Shadow, he left the apartment with a huge smile on his face, severely dehydrated. That encounter had been one for the books. One that Ghost would've been proud of. Shadow instinctively grabbed his cell phone to call his brother and give him all the dirty details, but quickly realized that he couldn't. There would be no more kinky tales that he could recount to his older brother in an attempt to impress him. There would be no more conversations between them of *any* kind, because Ghost was gone.

It had been four weeks since they'd laid Ghost to rest,

and Shadow felt his brother's absence every minute of every day. Ghost had been Shadow's idol. He was that nigga on the streets: Chancellor King's firstborn and the grand high executioner for the family. If you ran afoul of the Kings, you had to see Ghost. Yet this had nothing to do with why Shadow adored him so. To most who knew him, Ghost was a living nightmare who dispensed swift and brutal vengeance to enemies of the Monarchy; but to those who knew him intimately, Ghost was a loving son, an active father, and the best big brother Shadow could've ever wished for.

The circumstances surrounding Ghost's murder had been sketchy, to say the least. Ghost had been charged with executing a former gangster and current snitch who went by the name of Paul Schulman. Schulman had been responsible for framing Shadow's father Chancellor, the king of Five Points, for a murder he hadn't committed. Without Schulman's testimony, the police would likely have had to drop the conspiracy charges against Chance. Ghost had gotten rid of people at the behest of his father and the Monarchy before, but this was the first time Chance had ever given his son orders to kill directly. The king was desperate to get rid of Schulman, and his eldest son was the only person he truly trusted to get the job done.

According to Ghost's cousin Monster, the two of them had been ambushed on the way to carry out the hit, and Ghost was gunned down. Monster claimed that the shooters had been wearing masks, but the streets had already started talking. The chatter pointed to an associate of Shulman's, a low-level hustler who went by the name DeAndre. It had supposedly been DeAndre and a few of his boys who Schulman paid to take Ghost out. Monster had been able to track DeAndre down and promptly ended him, presenting his head in a box to Maureen King like a soldier handing a folded flag to the widow of a fallen comrade. The streets and the Monarchy had been satisfied with Monster's brutal execution of Ghost's alleged killer, but something didn't sit right with Ghost's mother Maureen or their associate Little Stevie, who proclaimed, "DeAndre was a lot of things, but a killer wasn't one of them. Even if he had been, there's no way a dipshit like him could've gotten the drop on Ghost."

Little Stevie and Maureen took their suspicions to the Monarchy, and demanded a full investigation into Ghost's murder, but the request was denied. As far as the Monarchy's Council of Lords was concerned, the murderer had been brought to justice and it was time to get back to business. Apparently, the old bastards who ran Five Points were more concerned about a dollar than their king being wrongfully imprisoned and the heir to the throne being murdered. Had Chancellor King still sat at the head of the table, he wouldn't have turned a blind eye to the child of one of his lords being murdered under questionable circumstances, but Chance was in prison fighting for his life and a new king now sat on the throne of Five Points.

A car horn brought Shadow out of the nightmare that he had been reliving, and his SUV inched forward. Traffic was unusually thick crossing the Pulaski Skyway toward the Holland Tunnel. It wasn't yet rush hour, though various construction projects were slowing things down. Shadow rode low in the seat of the truck—so low that it was a wonder he could see the road at all, but he managed. A manicured left hand gripped the steering wheel, while his elbow rested on the center console, a blunt of Sour pinched between his fingers. Shadow's body language said that he was feeling himself, but when wasn't he? His siblings called him a spoiled brat, always peacocking around like the world owed him a debt. Yet that wasn't it. Shadow's arrogance wasn't learned, or even practiced for that matter. It was just who he was, and he made no apologies for it.

Just ahead there was a break in traffic when a minivan carrying a family exited the 1 and 9 at the Holland Tunnel ramp in Jersey City. A white BMW that had been trailing the van hesitated, but Shadow didn't. As the BMW started to move forward, Shadow cut in front of it so close that the other driver had to jam on their brakes to avoid hitting him. The driver showed their displeasure by hitting their horn, to which Shadow replied by flipping them off before accelerating and weaving farther up the line of cars. The driver of the BMW was probably pissed, but Shadow didn't care. He was a King, and Kings didn't argue with peasants.

Traffic loosened up a bit as Shadow approached the Holland Tunnel. He killed his blunt and tossed it out the window. The weed was giving him cake-mouth. He reached toward the cup holder for a bottle of water and was disappointed to find it empty. There was another break in the traffic to his right and he swung into a BP gas station. He was at half a tank anyhow, and figured he'd kill two birds with one stone.

"Good afternoon," the gas station attendant greeted when Shadow pulled up to a pump.

"It sure is, ain't it?" Shadow pulled out his wallet and handed his debit card to the attendant. "Fill it up, and don't put none of that cheap shit in it. I'm watching you." He tapped his eyelid before ambling toward the gas station mart to grab something to drink.

"Asshole," the attendant mumbled, but not loud enough for Shadow to hear him.

Shadow stepped into the small store with the air of a property owner coming to collect two months of back rent. A young Arab woman behind the counter kept an eye on him as he headed to the back of the store. He had just grabbed a bottle of water when he happened to look out the window. The white BMW he'd cut off in traffic had just pulled into the station.

An eerie feeling overcame Shadow. He dipped behind a rack that held potato chips and pretended to be deciding which kind he was going to get, but he was actually checking the .25 he'd taken to carrying around with him. Shadow wasn't a shooter, but ever since Ghost's death, Maureen had insisted that no one in the family leave their house unarmed. Even if they were rolling with security, her children would be strapped at all times

Shadow pulled the chamber back to make sure one of the small projectiles was locked and ready, then slipped the gun into his front pocket and made his way to the register. He hardly heard a word the Arab woman said when she rang him up. The BMW was idling at the pump next to where Shadow had left his Benz, but wasn't getting gas. Shadow lingered in the store a bit longer, grabbing a pack of gum and a scratch-off. He wasn't sure if this was merely a coincidence or if the driver of the BMW had ill intentions, but his father had always taught him that it was best to receive bad news in person.

Shadow came out of the store absently rubbing a coin back and forth over the surface of the scratch-off. It was one of the large twenty-dollar tickets. Whether he won or not he couldn't say, because his eyes were still on the white car. As he neared his vehicle, the door of the BMW opened. His hand tightened around the .25, which he had hidden beneath the scratch-off.

To Shadow's surprise, a woman emerged from the BMW. She was light-skinned, possibly Hispanic, with long hair pulled back into a ponytail. She was wearing a white T-shirt that exposed a tattoo sleeve covering one of her shapely arms. The slacks she wore were a plain blue with a yellow stripe down the side, though they hugged her thick thighs like polyester leggings. Even before he spotted her polished boots, he knew the woman was either law enforcement or military. Her aggressive posture reinforced this impression. Confident that she wasn't an assassin, Shadow slipped the gun and scratch-off into his pocket.

"How you doing today, sis?"

"You know, that was some real bullshit you pulled back there, right?" Ms. Law Enforcement responded.

"What you mean?"

"Dude, I know you saw that you cut me off back there."

"I did? I'm so sorry, love. I been on the road all day and had to pee something terrible. I was paying more attention to where the closest gas station was than the cars around me. My apologies, Ms. Officer. You gonna write me a ticket or let me off with a warning?"

"I ain't police," she said. "I'm a CO at the Essex County jail."

"That's a shame, because I was hoping you had to write me a ticket so I could get your name."

"You don't need a ticket for all that. My name is Adelle."

"Like the singer?"

"No, like my granny. I was named after her."

"Well, it's nice to meet you, Adelle. My name is Shadow . . . Shadow King." He extended his hand and she accepted.

"Sounds like a comic book villain," Adelle joked.

"My name is Sean, but everyone calls me Shadow."

"Do I even want to know why?"

"It's a very interesting story. I can tell it to you over dinner."

"Boy, they would put me *under* the jail for fucking with your young ass. What are you, about nineteen . . . maybe twenty?"

"Actually, I recently had my twenty-first birthday," Shadow

lied; he was just shy of eighteen. "As long as we're two consent-ing adults, why should that matter? Don't cheat yourself out of something that could be potentially life-changing because you're worried about the court of public opinion."

"You talk a good game, Mr. Shadow," Adelle smirked.

"I *play* a better one, Ms. Adelle."

The woman sized him up. Shadow was clearly young, but he was also very handsome and so damn charming. It had been awhile since a man, young or old, had made Adelle feel *seen*. This included her baby's father, who currently occupied the couch in her apartment, from where he watched her pay all the bills around the house.

Shadow could see the conflict in Adelle's eyes. He had the fish on the hook, but knew he had to be careful about how he reeled it in for fear of losing it. "Look, I ain't trying to pressure you, sis. That ain't my style. Just let me put my number in your phone. If you use it, that's cool. If not, it was still a pleasure meeting you."

After a short pause, Adelle relented and handed over her phone. "Don't be trying to sneak and send yourself no Cash App from my phone either."

"C'mon, ma. I told you, my last name is King. That should tell you how I'm on it." Shadow returned her phone.

"Why do I feel like I've heard your name before?"

"You probably did—somewhere in the back of a beautiful dream about a brighter future."

"Sir," the gas station attendant called over to Shadow.

"Hold on, my man." He waved the man off and turned his attention back to Adelle. "I've eaten up enough of your time and I'm sure you've got shit to do. I hope to see you again, and maybe next time we can meet at someplace nicer than a gas station."

"We'll see. You drive safe out there, Shadow."

Shadow just stood there with a shit-eating grin as he watched Adelle slide back into her car. He imagined what that phat ass would look like without those slacks. When she turned back and caught him staring, he didn't bother to look away.

Adelle blushed and gave him a wave before pulling into traffic. She was acting like she wasn't sure if she was going to call, but Shadow knew that she would. He could tell in her eyes that it had been awhile since Adelle had been fucked properly. Shadow planned to change that. He'd always had a thing for older women, ever since one of his mother's friends had secretly given him blow job. Adelle checked all the boxes for his fetish: fine, thick, and gainfully employed. He was definitely trying to see what that was about.

"Sir!" the gas station attendant called to him again, this time with irritation in his voice. Shadow's car was blocking the only pump that wasn't currently in use.

"A'ight, nigga. Damn!" Shadow marched back over to his SUV. "You know, you could fuck up a wet dream. Where's my receipt? And I hope you didn't try and sneak none of that bull-shit gas in my ride when I wasn't looking."

"Your card got declined," the attendant told him.

"Say what?"

"Your payment—it didn't go through."

"Bullshit, I know that account is flush with cash!" The debit card he had given the attendant was linked to the joint account the siblings shared for emergencies and incidentals. Their parents always made sure there was at least twenty grand in that account. "Run it again."

"I ran it twice already. Look, maybe you have a different card you can pay with, or cash? Outside of that, I suggest you contact your bank. I'm not trying to be rude, but you're holding up traffic."

"Fuck you and this gas station!" Shadow snatched the card and jumped back in his Benz. There was obviously something wrong with their card reader, so Shadow would just go to another gas station when he got to Manhattan.

Sitting in traffic in the Holland Tunnel several minutes later, Shadow tried to log into his mobile banking app to see if he might've missed a fraud alert on the account. To his surprise, it flashed an error message and wouldn't allow him to log in. He tried again with the same result. He was about to try a third time when his phone rang. The initials *LS* followed by a gun emoji flashed across his screen.

"What's up with it?" At first there was no response. Shadow could hear commotion in the background and a woman yelling. "Hey, you there?"

"Sorry, kid," Little Stevie's voice finally came over the line. "There's a lot going on over here. Where are you right now?"

"Just coming from Jersey. Is everything okay? That sounds like Mom yelling in the back."

"You know I don't believe in sugar-coating shit, so no, everything is *not* okay. I need you to get back to the house ASAP."

CHAPTER 2

Shadow made it to the family mansion in Long Island in record time. Hearing his mother yelling was cause for concern, but what really had him rattled was the tone of Little Stevie's voice. He'd known his father's best friend his whole life and couldn't remember him ever being anything but a picture of cool.

When Shadow neared his home, he realized he had good reason to be concerned. He saw them before he even turned onto his block: blue and red flashing lights reflecting off the million-dollar homes. It seemed like all their neighbors were out on their front lawns or standing in the street, watching the spectacle. Shadow could count on one hand and still have fingers left the number of times he'd seen a police presence in this neighborhood since his dad had moved them there.

Shadow's heart thudded in his chest. In addition to the police cruisers, there were also several unmarked cars, a large moving truck, and two tow trucks, one of which was loading the prized King family limo onto a flatbed. Men wearing dark-blue windbreakers were coming out of the mansion carrying boxes filled with what looked like their personal items. It wasn't until Shadow pulled up to their circular driveway that he was able to read the lettering on the windbreakers, and when he did, he almost shit himself: *FBI.*

He left the car at the end of the driveway, behind one of the cruisers blocking it, and hurried toward the house. He found his mother standing in the doorway, dressed in a pink jogging suit and her house shoes, her hair wrapped in a silk scarf. Maureen's high-yellow brow was scrunched and fire burned in her hazel eyes. She was in the middle of a heated argument with one of the agents, while Little Stevie tried to calm her.

Another agent stepped out of the house carrying a box holding what looked like Chancellor King's office computer. Shadow's sister Lauren, or Lollipop as many people called her, was hot on the man's heels. Lolli was a shade darker than Maureen and had long black hair, which was pulled back into a ponytail. She was barking at the agent while trying to snatch something from the box. A female agent stepped between them and shoved Lolli back more aggressively than she needed to. Shadow sensed what was going to happen, and tried to move to stop it, but he wasn't fast enough. Lolli grabbed the female agent by the arm and flipped her to the ground. Lolli was a black belt in several different martial arts and could've finished the agent if she'd wanted to, but instead just held the woman on the ground, twisting her arm until she cried out in pain. Seconds later, two more FBI agents sprinted up and tackled Lolli.

"Get off my sister!" Shadow shouted, and charged at them. He had almost reached the struggling Lolli when one of the uniformed officers on the scene drew his gun and pointed it at Shadow.

"Don't make me do it to you, kid!" the officer warned. He was a young Black man, and his eyes said that he really didn't want to shoot Shadow, but his tight grip on the pistol said that he would.

"You crazy?" Shadow said. "You know who the fuck I am?"

"Yes, we know exactly who you and your family are, which is why we're here," replied an older FBI agent, a white man with thinning red hair and blue eyes. "Officer, I'm going to need you to lower that gun before you make a bad situation worse."

The uniformed cop was hesitant, but did as he was told.

"Take a walk," the older agent said. "And you two," he called to the agents wrestling with Lolli, "get off that young lady. We're law enforcement, not some damn savages."

"Tell that to *this* animal," one of the agents on the ground with Lolli replied.

"Bitch nigga, you got one more time to call my child anything but her Christian name and I'm gonna show the fuck out!" Maureen snarled.

The agents wisely, and silently, released their holds on Lolli.

"Maureen, please, we're——" the redhead agent began.

"That's *Mrs. King* to you. Don't be out here calling me by my first name like we're friends when y'all out here on some bullshit!"

"Okay, Mrs. King. We're just trying to do our jobs."

"Ma, what's going on?" Shadow cut in.

"A violation of our civil rights—that's what's going on," Lolli joined the conversation.

"This has nothing to do with civil rights. This is about ill-gotten gains," the redhead agent countered. "By order of a federal judge, this house, along with any other assets of Chancellor King, are to be seized."

Shadow spotted two men in coveralls at the end of the driveway preparing to hook his Mercedes to a tow truck. "Wait a damn minute! They can't take my truck, it was a graduation present."

"Likely purchased with money from one of your father's businesses, which are all currently under investigation," the agent said. "Listen, this is all very simple: If the King family can produce receipts and other proof that all this was obtained through legitimate income, then we can clear this up and be on our way. If not, you can try and buy it back when it goes to federal auction in thirty days. Now, if you'll excuse me . . ." He walked off to rejoin the other agents.

"Can they really do that?" Shadow said. "Take our house and everything in it?"

"According to *this* they can." Little Stevie read over the seizure warrant they'd been handed. "Since the feds came in and slapped those additional charges on your dad, on top of the alleged murder, they've been going over his financial records from the last two decades. They're trying to say that all this was bought with dirty money."

"Fuck that! I mean, we all know Daddy had one foot in and one foot out, but we have legal businesses too, like Second Chance Realty. There's no way he got all this with street money—right, Mom?" Shadow looked to Maureen for reassurance but found none. Her face was grim. Now it made sense why his card hadn't worked at the gas station: the feds had put a freeze on all their accounts.

Shadow stood on the lawn with his family watching as the agents loaded their whole lives onto the trucks and pulled off. The nail went into the coffin when two marshals attached a large lock to the front door and slapped a sticker across it, letting everyone know that the King home had been seized by order of the federal government.

"Peckerwood muthafuckas!" Little Stevie spat. "Don't you

fret, Maureen, I'm gonna get Chippie and the lawyers on this. We're gonna sue these bastards!"

Maureen nodded, but didn't respond. She watched with watery eyes as the last of the trucks pulled away with their property.

"They've taken everything," Shadow said. "What are we going to do now?"

Maureen turned her eyes to her two children, who were looking to her for answers—answers that she couldn't give them. But there was one thing she *did* know. "We do what Kings have been doing since the beginning of time: adapt and overcome."

CHAPTER 3

Several months later

Shadow found himself deep in a peaceful dream. He was reliving the fuck session he'd had with two white cheerleaders in high school. They were twins, Brittany and Barbie. Both girls were stacked, with fake tits, blond hair, and lip fillers. They came from a well-to-do family, with their mother being a lawyer and their dad a cop. Both parents were notoriously hard on Black folks whenever they had the chance, and never made a secret of their dislike for kids of a darker persuasion. This made the twins escape to the slums every chance they got to spite their parents, and most of the time Shadow would be there waiting for them with open arms.

The twins always felt like they had Shadow's nose open. Like he was one of those Black dudes who went sniffing around white tail whenever they got a little money. In truth, his fascination with the twins was a bit darker than that. Shadow made it a point that whenever he fucked one or both of them, he was punishing them for the sins of their father. Shadow was a rough lover by nature, as were most teenagers who hadn't yet learned how to properly throw their dicks, but he was especially cruel when it came to having sex with these twins. He defiled every one of their holes with his manhood, and when he fucked them in the ass, he never used lube. Shadow's dick would be raw for days afterward, but the discomfort was worth it to him for the privilege of violating the daughters of a cop and a prosecutor.

The night he was currently dreaming about had happened after their recent graduation. One of the rich kids they went to school with was having an afterparty at his parents' place in Englewood, New Jersey. Shadow and the twins had snuck off into one of the six bedrooms with three beans, a bottle of vodka, and a blunt of some killer weed that he had gotten from Pain. The girls were already drunk, so it didn't take long for the pills to kick in and Shadow found himself ass naked, tangled between them. He had Brittany bent over, burying dick in her, while Barbie was on her back between his legs, licking his balls. Every few seconds Shadow would slap Brittany hard across her ass and demand that she proclaim her love for Black dick.

"Yeah, baby . . . I love this Black dick! Fuck me like a project whore!"

Shadow was propped on one knee, drilling the hell out of Brittany, trying to push her intestines out through her mouth.

"Shit . . . shit . . . SHIT!" she cried out, climaxing and spraying both the bed and her sister's face.

"What the fuck, Britt?" Barbie rolled away, grabbing a sheet to wipe her face.

"I'm sorry, Sis . . . but his cock is so amazing," Brittany panted, while Shadow continued to stroke her.

"Then stop being such a greedy bitch and share!" Barbie pulled Shadow out of her sister, and pressed him down on his back.

Shadow beamed as Barbie climbed on top of him and rubbed her pussy against his dick before sliding him inside her.

Brittany's pussy was wetter, though Barbie's was warmer. It made him think about the first day of summer. Barbie was sexy as hell peering at him hungrily through chestnut eyes, her spill of dark hair brushing across his face every time she came down on him. Not wanting to be left out, Brittany snuggled up beside Shadow and started planting kisses on his chest, paying special attention to his nipples.

"Just like that," he urged Barbie. He put his head back and was enjoying the ride—until pain shot through his chest. Brittany had bitten his nipple hard enough to make him sit up. A thin trickle of blood ran down his chest. "D'fuck, bitch?"

"I'm sorry, baby, you just taste *so* good," Brittany said in a voice that was not her own. There was blood on her chin, which she licked away with an impossibly long tongue.

Shadow tried to shove Barbie off, but found himself pinned to the bed. The girl was 110 pounds soaking wet, but Shadow felt like he had the weight of a sumo wrestler on him.

"I want a taste too," Barbie sang, bearing fangs and a tongue identical to her sister's.

The twins descended on Shadow like two starved wolves, tearing off chunks of flesh and muscle while Shadow screamed into the night.

It was the screams. That's what had brought Shadow back from the dream . . . well, the nightmare, as it had turned out. Hearing his own voice ringing in his ears was what had rescued him from the horror of the demons devouring him alive. The dream had been so vivid that when Shadow awoke, he could still feel the pain in his chest from where Brittany had bitten him. His eyes darted around the room. There was a tall, expensive-looking mahogany dresser pushed against a wall with peeling green paint. Home Depot blinds covered in dust were pulled halfway down over the single window. The fantasy of the night in the six-bedroom house had faded and Shadow was back in his current reality. Graduation had come and gone, and instead of a beautiful white girl nibbling at his chest, Shadow found a large black rat. It was snacking on traces of whatever Shadow had fallen sleep eating.

"Shit!" Shadow knocked the rat away and jumped off the bed. He tried unsuccessfully to stomp it with his bare feet, but it escaped under the radiator in the corner. It wasn't the first time he had done battle with the black rat, and unfortunately, he knew it wouldn't be the last. "I fucking hate it here," he said aloud.

Shadow took a minute to compose himself, sitting on the edge of the bed with his head in his hands. The cheap linoleum floor was cold under his feet. Not like the heated tiles in his bedroom back at the mansion. In fact, nothing in his new home was the same as the mansion he and his family had been forced to vacate.

Shadow pushed to his feet and grabbed underwear from his dresser drawer. He put on his slides, then left his tiny bedroom and made his way toward an even smaller bathroom. He was happy to find it currently unoccupied. Unlike the King mansion, which had boasted five bathrooms, the apartment they now occupied had just one, which was shared by Shadow and his mother. Lolli, too, when she was there, so bathroom time caused a lot of friction in their home. Even so, having to shit and shower around each other's schedules was the least of the King family worries these days.

Shadow turned the shower on to let the water heat up while he took a leak. He had to do that sometimes because there was only one boiler supplying hot water throughout a building with eight apartments. When Shadow was done relieving himself, he stepped out of his boxers and into the shower. He was expecting a warm spray of water to help wash away the demons still clinging to him from the nightmare, but was instead greeted by a blast so cold that he jumped out of the shower and fell on his ass. Once again, the building's boiler was busted. It felt like the thing went out every two weeks. Had this happened at the King mansion, they'd have simply replaced the boiler instead of paying cheap laborers to perform temporary repairs. But the mansion was gone, and so was nearly everything else of value that Shadow and his family had once held precious.

He stayed there on the floor with his knees folded to his chest, thinking about how it all had gone so bad, so quick. When the one true king of Five Points fell, so did the kingdom he had built. Leaving Shadow and his mother buried beneath the rubble.

CHAPTER 4

Maureen King sat at the dining room table in the kitchen she had been forced to cook in over the past few months. It wasn't even a quarter of the size of kitchen she was used to moving around in, but it was all she had to work with now. Scattered across the table were legal documents, along with several receipts and invoices. She had been up since five a.m. crunching numbers and double-checking the fine print on contracts, yet her initial analysis kept coming back the same: they were fucked.

Long before her husband Chancellor's arrest, Maureen had seen it coming. He was a brilliant man, but so long as he kept his ties to the streets, the probability of the police one day kicking in their door had remained high. So she had prepared for this eventuality. At least as best she could. Maureen had cash squirreled away in various places, and had also made some very sound investments. She had invested in two food trucks and six ice carts that she spread across the city. The ice carts would bring in a shit-ton of cash during summers, and the food trucks would produce a moderate income all year round. The money they were already bringing in was decent, though not even close to what Second Chance Realty and some of their properties had generated before being seized.

The family had already been having a hard time fighting the bogus murder charge on Chance, and after the feds showed up at the mansion, things got considerably worse. They had slapped RICO and conspiracy charges on Chance. And once the king had been toppled, they sacked his kingdom. The government seized everything from their properties to their vehicles, and had frozen their bank accounts. Anything associated with Chancellor King or Second Chance Realty got snatched. The lawyers were fighting the good fight, but it appeared that the feds were planning to keep the King family finances tied up until hell froze over.

In addition to the money that came in from Maureen's smaller investments, Chance had also made sure she had a nice cushion to land on when she fell—though it wasn't enough to sustain her family long-term. Between paying for her husband's lawyers and the plush bed-and-breakfast they had to rent when the house was first seized, and also trying to keep up appearances, that cushion was flattening. It would only be a matter of time before Maureen's finances bled out. Sacrifices would have to be made for the family to weather the storm. It stung when Maureen had to sell off most of her jewelry and designer clothes, but those were material items that she was certain she could get back once all this was over. The real blow came when she had to tell her family that they were moving back to Brooklyn.

The sole property that the government hadn't been able to seize was one of Chance's first major purchases: the apartment building in Bed-Stuy. A few years prior, Chance had transferred ownership of it into a trust for Shadow. Maureen initially wanted to sell the building for some quick cash, but there was no telling how long Chance's case would drag out.

After quite some debate, she decided that the most economical decison would be to move into the walk-up. It was supposed to be a temporary situation—at least that's what she told herself. And now, with Chance's case moving at a snail's pace, she was glad that they hadn't sold the building; it looked like they might be there for some time.

"Good morning, Ma," Shadow said as he entered the kitchen.

"Hey, Son." Maureen gathered the papers into a messy pile in front of her so that Shadow couldn't read them. "Was that you I heard yelling?"

"Nah. Might've been Lolli. You know she suffers from really bad nightmares."

"When she actually sleeps." Maureen shook her head. "Girl roams the streets at all kinds of ungodly hours. And those rare nights when she does stay here, she don't do nothing but pace the house all night like the damn ghost of Christmas past. I'm starting to worry about her. She ain't been right since all this foolishness started with your dad."

Lolli had indeed been a bit off lately. She was never what one would consider normal—she was a thrill seeker who was always putting herself in dangerous situations, that's how she got her kicks—but there had been a noticeable change in her since their father had been locked up. She had started drinking heavily, and doing things that were out of character, like going missing for days at a time and getting into bar fights. Maureen assumed that Lolli was just suffering through depression due to the arrest of her father and the death of her brother Ghost, but the young woman's issues ran even deeper.

What nobody other than Shadow knew was that Lolli blamed herself for what had happened to her father. It was she who had gone after Alderman James Porter when he refused to back her father. Lolli admitted to roughing him up during her second visit with him, but swore that he had been alive when she left. Someone else had killed him and framed their dad for the murder, and Lolli had become obsessed with finding out who. She now spent most of her evenings drinking and roaming the streets like a predator. Shadow feared that his big sister was coming unglued.

"No school today?" Maureen asked.

"Nah, we're on break," Shadow lied again.

"Seems like y'all always on a break."

"This is college, Ma, not high school. Totally different set of rules." In truth, Shadow hadn't seen the inside of a classroom in two weeks. On top of everything else he was dealing with, a tuition payment to Pace University was now overdue. Monster had given him a few dollars and even Pain had chipped in something, but it wasn't enough. Shadow wanted to ask his mother if she could make up the difference, but knew they weren't exactly flush with cash at the moment. He decided to change the subject: "Oh, the hot water is busted again."

"Damn it! I just paid to have it repaired a few weeks ago. I'm gonna call them Mexicans to come back out here. They'll either do the job right or give me the money back."

"Instead of continuing to patch up the old one, why don't we just invest in a new one?"

"Because it's money that we don't have right now. We're barely getting by on the bit of change your dad left and from my trucks on the streets."

Shadow thought on the dilemma for a moment. "Maybe we can just pull it from the rent money?"

"Boy, please." Maureen sucked her teeth. "Them few pennies these tenants are paying are barely enough to keep the building from collapsing, let alone perform any upgrades. And before you ask, no, we can't go up on it. Your daddy, bless his foolish heart, made an agreement that he wouldn't go up on the rent. Even when every other property owner took advantage of gentrification, your daddy kept the rent here the same."

"Dad is a smart businessman, but that doesn't sound like a wise move," Shadow said.

"The arrangement had more to do with your father and his damn sense of nobility than business. Chance always said that Black folks in the city were already living under oppressive conditions and he didn't want to add to the load they were carrying, so he did the residents of his building a kindness with the fixed rent. This applied only to the tenants who were already in here at the time. For as long as they lived in one of these apartments, they'd never have to worry about him going up on the rent. Even when the other property owners got the city involved and tried to force Chance to raise the rent, he stood firm."

"Damn, that was gangsta."

"I'm sure he thought so too, but it was a fool's move and one of the few he didn't consult me on before he made it. Folks in Brooklyn are paying three grand a month to live in a shoebox apartment with a shared bathroom. Do you know how much I could rent a two-bedroom unit to one of them white yuppies in today's housing market? Your daddy trying to be Robin Hood done put us behind the eight ball at a time when we need every damn dollar we can put our hands on." Maureen sighed. So far, she had managed to keep them afloat by squeezing blood from stones, but her hands were starting to hurt. She wasn't sure how much longer she could keep this up.

It physically pained Shadow to see his mother looking so defeated and knowing there wasn't a whole lot he could do about it. He sat in the chair beside her and did the only thing he could think to do at the moment: rub her back. "It's gonna be okay, Ma. Trouble don't last."

"I know, baby, but that bitch Trouble has certainly over-stayed her welcome."

"Ma, I . . ." Shadow's words trailed off.

"What, Son? What were you going to say?"

Shadow had an idea, though he had to be mindful of how he phrased it. "You know it doesn't have to be like this, right? Us fending for ourselves like we ain't got people we can turn to."

"Shadow, don't . . ."

"Why not? Dad is in prison, but the show is still going on. When I saw Monster after graduation, he told me that if we needed anything, we should come see him or Uncle Chapman. Ain't like we're looking for handouts. This is what's owed to us . . . what's owed to Daddy."

"Shadow, you don't understand." Shadow was a good son, but he was also a naïve son. Of all Maureen's children, he was the only one who couldn't seem to see the animals for the jungle.

"What I don't understand is why we have to live in the ghetto and nobody else does. We're Kings!" Shadow slapped his chest. "The only thing standing between us and the poverty line is the queen and her pride."

Maureen looked up at her youngest child, chest poked out and eyes burning with a fury that he believed would give him the strength to save not only his family, but the whole world. Shadow was much like his father in that way: noble, honorable. He would forever see himself as the white knight in whatever cause he was trying to champion—until someone knocked him off that horse and he found himself covered in mud. Well, if her son was determined to wallow in the dirt, she would be the one to throw the first handful on him.

Maureen didn't answer him right away. She got up and went to the kitchen cabinet, where she grabbed a bottle of Hennessy and two coffee mugs. She placed one mug in front of Shadow and poured two fingers in each. Shadow looked down at the liquor, not sure where she was going with this.

"So, you think you old enough to finally have a real conversation?" Maureen began. "I'm gonna give it to you, but you gonna need that yak to numb some of the pain that's gonna come with it."

Shadow accepted the mug and took a small sip. It stung his lips and throat like liquid fire. It wasn't the first time he'd had Hennessy—he drank it often when he was out with Pain—but there was something about his mother watching him over the rim of her own glass that seemed to make it burn a little hotter than usual.

"If you think something like what you're suggesting would even be an option for Maureen King, then you know even less about who I am than I feared. Whether the king is at my side or not, I am still the queen. Your father's throne wasn't even cold yet when that snake brother of his crawled his prissy ass into it. That seat should've gone to Ghost, and when he died, it should have gone to *you* by default. That thirsty bastard Chapman jumped the line of succession and those disloyal bastards who call themselves the Monarchy let him! Chapman is a piece of shit, but Chance was always a good little brother to him, even when he didn't deserve the king's mercies. Bad enough he snuck his way to the head of the table, but you'd have thought that when he got there, he'd have done the right thing. Has he?"

Shadow stayed quiet.

"Of course not. Chapman played the concerned brother only long enough to figure out how good a shot your father had at beating this case. When things got dark, your Uncle Chapman got missing. I'd crawl over glass to punch the clock at a manure farm before I accepted anything from your uncle, except for his traitorous head."

Chapman's jealousy over his younger brother inheriting the throne from their father was no secret. His scheming on the crown had been constant, but as long as Ghost was around to succeed Chance in the event that something happened, Chapman had to suffer in silence. Chance being arrested and Ghost dying had given Chapman the window he needed to swoop in and stake his claim. It had all lined up too perfectly, and Maureen never felt like it had been a coincidence. She knew that Chapman's fingerprints were on this disaster somewhere, she just didn't know where.

"Ma, I know who and what Uncle Chapman is. He always felt some type of way about Daddy. But if we sat with him . . . maybe we could figure something out that works for everybody? When I was talking to Monster, he said—"

"Fuck that melon-head freak of nature too!" Maureen cut Shadow off. "You think I don't see the way he's implanted himself up Chapman's ass since Ghost was killed? Up until a few months ago, the two of them couldn't stand each other, but all of a sudden they've mended their uncle-nephew bond? I call bullshit on the whole thing! I wouldn't put it past Monster to have had a hand in what happened to my C.J.," she said, referring to Chancellor Junior—Ghost's government name.

"Chapman being disloyal to the family . . . I could see that. But Monster? He loved Ghost more than anybody."

"Nobody loved C.J. more than me, so let me stop you there. Sean, I know you always try and see the good in everyone, but I'm about to say some things that you're probably not gonna like, but really need to hear. I know you're my *good* son, the kid who never disappoints his mother, but considering what you were raised around, I find it hard to believe that you're seriously that green. You think for one minute that a muthafucka who ain't got shit won't step on somebody else who they feel has too much just so that they can get a little bit of something? It can be your best friend, or your family. No matter how noble a man professes to be, deep down he knows the exact dollar amount it would take to purchase his soul. Monster would cut his own mama's head off and take it to a pawnshop if he felt like he could get a coin out of it. In this life of ours, we're constantly surrounded by the worst of the worst. I'm not judging, because Lord knows this family has buried more than its share of bones. Your father might have inherited the crown from his daddy, as was the way of the King men, but he *built* this kingdom. And when he did, it was blood and bodies that provided the foundation."

"Ma, I know the history of this family—probably better than you give me credit for. I try and stay away from those kinds of conversations with you, because I know how hard you and Dad worked to keep me out of that side of the family business."

"That was your daddy." Maureen took a sip from her mug, appreciating the liquor's burn before continuing. "Ghost was your father's heir, but honestly, that's where the buck stopped as far as his qualifications for sitting on the throne. I loved my son, but he was more of a warlord than a king. His skill set would've better served this family by succeeding your Uncle Colt as commander of the Reapers, rather than my husband as king."

This confession surprised Shadow. The Reapers were the stuff of legends, an elite death squad loyal only to the king of Five Points and commanded by Chancellor's younger brother Colt. Colt had been Shadow's favorite uncle. With his father often busy with affairs of the Monarchy or chasing his political aspirations, Shadow had spent a great deal of time with Uncle Colt. The man taught Shadow a lot—not just about the game, but about being a man. Like Ghost, Colt had met with a violent end under dubious circumstances. He had been found in his car with a single gunshot wound to the head. The police had written it off as a robbery gone bad, but at the time of his death, Colt had been wearing at least thirty thousand dollars' worth of jewelry and all of it was accounted for. Ever since Colt's death, Shadow had been plagued with nightmares, often about his uncle. Things had gotten so bad at one point that his parents put him in therapy to try to help him deal with the trauma.

"You ever share this with Dad? Your reservations about Ghost being king?" Shadow asked.

"A time or three," Maureen answered. "Once Chance's mind was made up about something, there was really no changing it. As was the case where you were concerned. Your role in this family was something that your father and I always agreed to disagree on."

"How so?" The liquor was making Maureen talkative and Shadow wanted to use the opportunity to gain insight on things they rarely spoke about.

"Your dad had a particular vision for his children. Millie was already turned out, Ghost had a natural nose for the streets, and Lolli was just Lolli. Those three were going to be who they were regardless of how we felt about it, and that's something that always haunted your dad. He felt like he didn't do a good enough job saving them from themselves, and vowed to not make that same mistake with his baby boy. In you, he saw what his own life and the lives of his other children could never be—untainted. You were the perfect block of clay for him to mold as he wanted. I respected him wanting to do right by you, but I also knew it would be a fool's errand. From the day each one of my kids came into the world and I looked into y'all eyes for the first time, I understood what your true natures would be."

"And what did you see my true nature would be, Ma?" Shadow took a gulp from his mug. He was starting to feel the brown liquor.

"You? You're a conqueror. No, you might not have been out there gobbling up territory like Ghost, or knocking off business competitors like Lolli, but you're the damn Pied Piper when it comes to getting people to do what you want. Take these young whores you keep time with, for example. I used to get embarrassed for some of these young girls who let you manipulate them. And it ain't just the women. Look at Fresh and Pain, how they would follow you through hell's gates without thinking twice."

"Fresh and Pain are my boys. As for the ladies, you know your son got game."

"What you're undervaluing as simple game, I call a skill set that will serve you well if you apply it properly. Sean, you're using your God-given talents for the wrong shit. Petty shit. Boy, you have the rare ability to convince folks to do things, even when they know it ain't no good for them. You can't teach that or learn it. You have to be born with it, like I was. How you think your daddy got to where he did so fast? Chance plowed the fields, but your mama planted the seeds. That's your gift, boy . . . natural qualities of a king."

This was a side of his mother that Shadow wasn't used to seeing, so he wasn't sure what to make of it, though it felt good to finally hear her acknowledge his capabilities. He had always felt lacking when measured against his siblings, so this was high praise.

"I don't knock your dad for how he chose to raise you,"

Maureen continued, "but had it been up to me, you would've been out in the world with Ghost collecting battle scars. So that when and if the time came for you to step up, you'd be able to take a punch."

"I can take a punch pretty good, Ma. But you and Dad never let me end up in a position to get hit. I always wanted to be more for this family."

"Then now is your chance to make it so."

"How? Dad is locked up and Uncle Chapman is the new king. What can I do?"

"Take back what belongs to *us*," Maureen said flatly. "How Chapman came to power was some bullshit. We know it and so do the streets. There are some who feel just as strongly as us about not wanting to follow a false king—but he's the only game in town right now. Only way to right Chapman's wrong is to give the Monarchy a better option."

Shadow couldn't hide his shock at what his mother was suggesting. It was common knowledge among the family that he was the least suited to carry on the King legacy, and here was his mother asking him to do something that they both knew wasn't in his nature. Shadow had gotten used to being the kid upon whom they placed the least expectations, yet the winds of change were blowing.

"Ma, I'm not Ghost."

Maureen kissed him on the forehead. "I know that, and hopefully *they* will too."

CHAPTER 5

"Cleaned them boys up!" Cheese declared. He was looking absently in the rearview mirror while picking at the acne on his light-skinned face. It was a habit he'd had since he was a kid, and it had left him with acne scars.

"Say, word?" John responded from the passenger seat of the Ford sedan. He was putting the finishing touches on a blunt he was rolling as he listened to Cheese recounting the details of a home invasion he'd missed out on.

"I can't lie, I was a little disappointed," Cheese said. "We all heard the stories about his team being about that, but once they seen what we did to the bitch, they laid down without too much of a fight."

"I still can't believe Christian went against the grain like that. He a little weird, but never struck me as no traitor. He always seemed down for the team." John didn't really know Christian personally, but he had seen him around and knew he was a lieutenant in the King organization.

"Christian wasn't never loyal to nobody but himself. Sure, Ghost built him up and gave him a purpose other than taking dick—but how did Christian repay him? Ghost wasn't even cold in the ground before Christian tried to lay claim to what he hadn't earned. He'd been sucking Ghost's dick for so long that he thought when the big homie got murdered, he would inherit the empire like some grieving fucking widow. He tried to jump the line instead of respecting the pecking order, and now his ass is on Monster's shit list."

"That ain't a list I'd want to be on," John said. "That ugly muthafucka Monster gives me the creeps."

"Yeah, Monster's with the shits, but he's all brawn and no brains. The only reason I haven't killed him for laying his hands on me is because Judah told me to stand down—but best believe I ain't letting it go." Cheese touched the scar under his eye: a gift from the man in question a few months earlier. Cheese had made the mistake of making an off-color joke about Ghost's fiancée and it didn't go over well. Monster's thrashing was the closest Cheese had ever come to death, and like the scar, he still carried the memory with him.

"If I were you, I'd just charge that one to the game, big bruh, and leave Monster the fuck alone," John said. "I heard when he found the kid who laid Ghost down, he cut the dude's head off with a chain saw."

"Stop being so quick to believe everything you hear," Cheese responded.

"You trying to say that didn't happen?"

"What I'm saying is, some things are better left undiscussed."

It was true, Monster had indeed separated a man's head from his body and presented it to the queen as the murderer of her son. But Ghost's actual killers were not only still alive, they were eating off the plate he had left behind. The only thing poor DeAndre had ever killed in his life was a bottle of liquor. His death had been a necessary sacrifice and the only thing that had prevented an all-out war in the streets. There was no way that the lords of the Monarchy, or the Kings for that matter, were going to rest with Ghost's murder going unsolved. They would keep digging until they found something, and there was too much at stake for the new powers that be to let that happen. So, DeAndre was offered up to pacify the grieving family and the organization. In the end, DeAndre should've considered it an honor that he died to preserve something greater than he would ever be.

"So, you think Christian is gonna try and get back at the niggas for running up in his spot and killing two of his?"

"One of them was a fiend, so she don't count. The other nigga?" Cheese shrugged. "If that dick-smoker Christian has any sense in that processed head of his, he'll get in line under this new regime like everyone else. I was hoping he'd be in the apartment when we busted in so that I could've personally put a bullet in his head, but his time is coming. Bet that."

"If I were you, I wouldn't take Christian lightly," John said. "I hear that boy is hella dangerous, despite his appearance."

Cheese laughed. "It'll be a cold day in hell before a nigga prancing around in heels and makeup gets the better of me. Killing him is gonna be my pleasure. I never did like that pretty muthafucka!"

The running banter in the hood about Christian revolved around his sexuality. Christian carried himself in a whimsical manner, and was always outrageously dressed. Behind his back, the soldiers referred to him as "Twink," and it was a blow to Cheese's pride when he found out that Twink had slept with his child's mother. When word started to spread, Cheese found himself the butt of a great many jokes, and he had never quite gotten over the embarrassment.

"What the fuck y'all doing in here besides slipping?" a third voice joined the conversation, startling Cheese and John. The man was standing just short of the driver's-side window, peering into the vehicle. He was wearing a simple black Nike sweat suit and a single silver chain which bore the Star of David. Though his government name was Judah Friedman, many simply referred to him as the Black Jew. His family lineage could supposedly be traced back to the fourth son of Jacob from the Bible. At least indirectly.

Growing up, religion had no place in Judah's heart. To him, no god of any faith would have allowed him and his mother to suffer as they had. This changed when Judah's mother met the man who changed not only their lives but also their names. Herman Friedman came from a family of Realtors, but was known to keep his beak wet in the streets. Two things he taught young Judah after he married his mom were the Torah and how to flip a dollar. Herman was one of the few men Judah had ever met who showed him love, so he embraced both his stepfather and the Jewish faith. Judah would sometimes find himself shunned when he attended temple with Herman. Though it stung, he continued to go because it was where he and his stepdad bonded. It was their thing. Even after Herman Friedman passed away, his stepson continued to follow this path—with a few detours along the way.

Judah held some sway on the streets, though he hadn't always. He'd started out as a dusty stickup kid who went out robbing just so he could eat. But once the robbery game got his weight up, Judah turned his attention to weight of a different kind. It started out with Judah and Cheese buying ready-rock from a middleman, and before long they were purchasing weight from an associate of the King family. They were good at flipping work, which is what eventually put them on Ghost's radar. Ghost had offered to open up the market for them, though he needed something done in return. It was a petty request, one that Judah had reservations about honoring, yet he needed what Ghost and his family brought to the table. So he did what had been asked of him, but he never looked at Ghost the same afterward. Ironically enough, it was this task that inadvertently set the wheels in motion that led to Ghost's murder.

"Damn, nigga!" Cheese barked. "Make some noise when you walk. I didn't even hear you roll up."

"That's because y'all too busy in here gossiping like two high school girls instead of being on point," Judah scolded. "What were y'all in here talking about anyhow that was so deep you let a nigga get close enough to blow your brains out?"

"Just some bullshit," Cheese said. "What's good with you though? I'm surprised you not running with the big man today." Judah and Monster had become thick as thieves once they started working together, and Cheese didn't like it. He and Judah had been best friends since they were shorties.

"Monster's attending to something above both our pay grades right now, but I'm meeting up with him later to secure that other thing we discussed—with the Cubans."

"Word? Count me in! You see the way that girl was looking at me last time? I think she wants to fuck. I'm about to try and crack that." Cheese rubbed his hands together remembering his encounter with the beautiful Cuban girl, Josette. He met her in passing one day while riding with Monster and Judah to handle something for her family, who were in the life.

"Josette Zaza is a flirt who gets off on waving her pussy at niggas and watching them get whacked when they reach for it," said Judah. "Let that shit go, homie, and let's stay focused on business."

Cheese was a pussy hound, but Orlando Zaza's youngest daughter was a black widow. She liked to play dangerous games.

Judah knew this firsthand because he had almost gotten caught up. The pussy was good, though not worth the headache that came when the shit hit the fan. The only reason Judah was still breathing was because of his standing in the new King organization and the fact that the two families needed each other. It was a lesson that he only needed to learn once, and he wasn't going to let any of his people enroll in her class of bullshit.

"Cock-blocking-ass nigga," Cheese joked. "So if you ain't gonna let me get to the pussy, I assume you're about to put me on the money?"

"Something like that," Judah said. "I might need you to put in some pain."

"Just tell us whose wig gotta get split and we on it!" John chimed in. They had almost forgotten he was even sitting in the car until he opened his mouth. John hadn't been running with the crew for very long, though he was eager to prove that he belonged. He had been relegated to grunt work so far, but he longed for the day when he would find himself in a position to prove himself to Judah.

Judah ignored him. "Cheese, jump out for a minute so I can holla at you." He walked off without waiting to see if Cheese would follow. "What's wrong with that kid, he retarded or something?" Judah asked once they were out of John's earshot.

"Don't pay him no mind," Cheese said. "He's young and eager to impress, that's all."

"Well, you better get him in line. This is an army, not no fucking circus. Doing clown shit will get that boy hurt out here." Judah moved quietly and didn't like people who were impulsive or attracted attention, which always seemed to be the case with John. He would've cut him loose already had Cheese not been so fond of the guy.

"I'll talk to him," Cheese responded. "So, what's the next move?"

"It appears that our sugary friend has received our message, but still refuses to play nice. So it's time for us to speak to him in a language that he better understands." Judah pulled up his sweatshirt so Cheese could see his gun.

"Yeah, that's what I'm talking about. We gonna run up in his club with the gang and bang him, or catch him while he's with one of his whores?"

"*We* ain't gonna do shit. This is on you, Cheese."

"Hold up . . . you sending me at him by myself?" Cheese knew just who and what he was dealing with when it came to the so-called Prince of the Night.

"Monster wants this done right and quietly. If you think you ain't up to the task, I can give it to somebody else. Maybe the young boy who been running with us? He's already showed that he ain't scared to bust his gun." Judah was referring to their latest recruit, a young dude who had ended up in their fold by accident. He didn't look like a killer, but when his number was called, he hadn't hesitated. Judah had been contracted by Ghost King to kill another dealer who called himself Malice. Judah had every intention on laying Malice down, but the young man had beat him to it. Judah wanting to take care of Malice had been about business, but for the young man it was personal. Cheese had suggested they kill the kid because he wasn't really one of them and had been involved in the murder, but Judah vetoed the idea. The kid wasn't street-poisoned like the rest of them, though under Judah's tutelage, he soon would be.

"The lil pretty nigga?" Cheese said. "Fuck outta here. He ain't even been with us six months, and I been down since the beginning. No way you're gonna let that wet-behind-the-ears nigga steal my glory. I *got* this."

"Then act like it. Now, I want to off Christian outright, but for some reason Monster seems to think it's a good idea to keep giving him chances at redemption. Be as forceful as you need to be to get him to see eye to eye with us, but Monster would prefer you don't kill him."

"I don't work for Monster. What *you* think?"

Judah considered this for a moment. "I think it'd be in your best interest to follow Monster's orders to the letter, but if something happens and Christian ends up a stain on the sidewalk, whatever he had becomes ours. Feel me?"

"Indeed I do." Cheese smiled.

CHAPTER 6

After talking with his mother for a bit about her expectations of him, Shadow slipped outside. He didn't have any classes that morning and was supposed to be going on a job interview, but after the heavy conversation he'd had with Maureen, punching a clock no longer seemed so appealing to him. Instead, he parked his ass on the front steps of the building and fired up a blunt while he tried to figure it all out.

Nobody could apply pressure to their children like Maureen King. She had a way about her that made them feel like they were being disloyal anytime they disagreed with something she said or did. She never showed her displeasure outright; it was always subtle: a sideways glance, an off-handed comment, or utter silence. Regardless, you'd know the queen wasn't happy and you'd go out of your way to try to make it right. Maureen could make a fish think it was drowning. It was what happened with Ghost that one fleeting moment when he'd considered going straight: Maureen had convinced him that his father would be lost without him. Lolli had wanted to be a painter, but Maureen forced her into espionage.

Prior to Chancellor King being arrested, Shadow's life had

been all mapped out. He would finish high school, go off to college to earn a degree, and when he was ready, he'd fill Chancellor's shoes running the King family's legitimate businesses. Sadly, those dreams ended up being deferred. With their finances depleted, the prospect of making it all the way through college was starting to feel more and more far-fetched. The family needed money, and Shadow had offered to go get a job so he could help out during these troubled times. To this, Maureen had replied: "I'd rather sell my body on a street corner than have a member of the royal family degrade themselves by flipping burgers or pushing a mop."

Behind Shadow, the front door of the building opened. He tried to hide the blunt, thinking that it was his mother. She knew he smoked weed, but out of respect he never let her see him doing it.

From the building emerged a well-built Black man. A neatly trimmed goatee covered his chin and a red, black, and green kufi was pulled snugly over his head.

"Morning, Shadow."

"Morning, Mussa."

Mussa was an ex–drug dealer and addict who had discovered Islam while in prison. He spotted the blunt in Shadow's hand and frowned. "How many times have I asked you not to sit here smoking that, man? You know we got these babies running in and out of the building. Put a little shade on your vice."

"My fault." Shadow stubbed the blunt out. In the few years since he'd been out of prison, Mussa had spent a lot of his time trying to undo some of the damage he'd done in the community when he'd been out running wild and reckless. It was a thankless job, but Shadow respected Mussa because no matter how lopsided the battle, the man never stopped fighting. He was much like Shadow's dad in that way.

"What you doing out here at this time of day anyhow?" Mussa asked. "You should be in class around this time."

"School is cancelled."

Mussa had a niece who attended Pace University too, and knew for a fact that she had classes that day. He was going to point this out to Shadow, but picked up on the fact that the young man was in a dark mood and switched topics: "I saw your sister Millie the other day. She looks good too, respectfully."

"Sixty-three days clean, according to her." Shadow knew this because every time she came by, she made it a point to mention how many days sober she had under her belt.

"That's quite an accomplishment, considering how far out there she got at one point. You should celebrate her for that, but that's not what I'm getting from you."

"What, you want us to throw her a party for not doing something she shouldn't have done in the first place?" Shadow chuckled.

"Spoken like a man who's never had something he couldn't control strip him of everything he values."

Shadow craned his neck to look up at Mussa. "Do you not see where we've been forced to live?" The minute the words left his mouth, Shadow regretted them. After all, Mussa was also a resident in his father's slum building. "I meant no disrespect," he added.

"And I took none from it." Mussa hiked up his jeans and took a seat on the steps next to Shadow. "Do you remember the last time me and you chopped it up on this stoop? And what we talked about?"

"You mean last week when you were talking shit about my Brooklyn Nets?" Shadow and Mussa always got into it over sports.

"Nah, man. We both know it'll only ever be one true New

York basketball team, and they don't play in Kings County. It's Knicks or nothing! But seriously, I mean that time awhile back when we discussed what it meant for a junkie to hit their bottom."

Shadow indeed recalled the conversation. He'd been fooling around in the city with his best friends Pain and Fresh, and they were about to go up into the old apartment. This was before it had once again become the mailing address for the King family. At that time, it was still just an empty apartment that Chancellor kept as a reminder of where he had come from, which Shadow used like clubhouse to smoke weed and sleep with women whenever he was in the area. Mussa had dropped some heavy jewels on him that afternoon. Jewels which had ended up proving their worth that very same night.

Shadow looked Mussa in the eye. "You think Millie finally hit her bottom?"

"You got a better explanation about the one-eighty she's done with her life? It's like I told you back then, Shadow: the only person who can help a junkie is a junkie."

"Ain't like we didn't try."

"I don't doubt that, but you still ain't listening. Didn't matter how much money your people had, or what kind of treatment you could've provided for Millie, for her to kick before she was ready. Her *ah-ha* moment hadn't come yet. And sadly, for most addicts those moments don't come until they've been put in situations where they've almost lost their lives, or are in their final moments. I don't even wanna think about what Millie might've gone through to bring her to the point where she's ready to turn it around, but I thank Allah she's still here to receive that second chance. I know in your eyes you see your sister as weak for getting strung out, and I can understand why you may feel that way. Most people look at addicts like they're shit on a shoe, and forget they were real, everyday people just like you before getting caught up. You don't know what Millie might've gone through that made her turn to the pipe. I don't expect you to factor in these kinds of things, because you ain't never been caught in the throes of that demon. So your perception is one-sided. Getting hooked on something is easy, but finally being able to break the hold it has over you without dying or going to prison is akin to an act of God. If I had to guess, I'd say Millie is far stronger than you've been giving her credit for. Try to cut her a little slack here and there, young blood."

"I hear you, OG."

"Don't just hear me, Sean, *listen* to what I'm saying."

Shadow let Mussa's words sink in. He was no stranger to addicts—his family being tied so heavily to the streets, he had been around them all his life. All Shadow had ever seen growing up were the dope boys treating addicts like they were sub-human, so that's how he'd always perceived them. Now, here was Mussa giving him a different perspective. Millie was his half sister, the product of a relationship his mother had been in before meeting his father. Millie wasn't that much older than the children Chancellor and Maureen had together, but she had been getting high for as long as Shadow could remember. This meant that she had been out there from an early age.

Shadow tried to look past the addict he had been introduced to as his older sister, and began to wonder what Millie had suffered through to turn her to drugs so young. Had his father pressured her—like his mother was now doing with him—to be something she didn't want to be, and she simply folded under it, or had something happened to her that pushed Millie over the edge?

"Oh, and you might want to mention to your mom that the hot water is out again," Mussa said.

"She knows. She said she gonna try and find somebody to take care of it as soon as she can."

"Why doesn't your mom hire someone to take care of the upkeep of the building instead of picking up random Mexicans outside the Home Depot who ain't gonna do shit but slap a Band-Aid on the problem?" Mussa laughed, but Shadow stayed silent. "You know I was only messing with you, right?"

"I know, Mussa. It ain't you. Things are just a little crazy for us right now on the financial side."

Mussa understood without Shadow having to elaborate. He, too, knew how it was to have your family bleed themselves dry trying to fight a criminal case. His mother had lost her house when she put it up for his bond and he skipped on it. It remained one of Mussa's biggest regrets. "Tell you what. Maybe we can come to some type of arrangement that works for everyone. I got my carpenter's certificate when I was in prison. I'm no expert, but I know my way around a hammer. Maybe I can take care of some of the minor repairs that need to be done around this place?"

"Mussa, I just told you that money is tight. We got no way to pay you right now."

"Then you can compensate me in trade. Maybe take a little something off the rent every month in exchange for my services?"

"We don't need no charity, Mussa."

"This ain't charity, it's the barter system. No pressure, just know that I'm here." Mussa laid a hand on Shadow's shoulder.

"Thank you." Shadow was trying to keep his emotions in check. He was so used to his family helping everybody else and didn't quite know how to accept it when the tables were turned.

Before the conversation could go any further, their attention was drawn to what sounded like a gunshot. They were on their feet in an instant, with Mussa putting himself between Shadow and the potential danger. They heard the sound again—getting closer. The third time they heard it, they figured it was just a car backfiring—until they saw it bend the corner. It had the basic construct of a motorbike—two wheels, handlebars, and a seat—but this smoking, coughing, wheezing thing was a jumble of metal, plastic, and rubber, ridden by someone just as twisted. When it came to a sputtering stop in front of the Brooklyn tenement, the rider removed his helmet. He was dark and handsome, wearing his hair in starter-kit braids tied off with rubber bands. His slim frame was swallowed by an oversized, matte-gray leather jacket. Embroidered just above the right breast was a murder of black crows flying in a circle around a bloodstained bullet.

Shadow wasn't familiar with the symbol, but he knew the rider. "That son of a bitch can't be street legal," Shadow said with a grin as the man dismounted. "Ain't no state where it'd pass an emissions test."

"When you ever known me to let the laws of state or man dictate how I move?" The rider gave Shadow dap. This was Pain, Shadow's best friend and one of the only people who had been consistent in his life.

Pain represented one third of Shadow's little crew; the other was their friend Fresh. Together, they were like the Three Amigos, though Shadow and Pain had always been closest. Their friendship went back to when they were both children standing in the shadows of dangerous men. Shadow and his family had still been living in Brooklyn in those days. Pain hadn't been heavy in the game yet, he was just a runner for one of Ghost's lieutenants. His duties had been limited to small things like watching over drug packages in the stash houses, or holding guns when the homies were out on the block. Shadow had spent a lot of time in that period with his Uncle Colt, who had a small operation he ran out of Harlem. That was where Shadow first crossed paths with a young Pain. Whereas Shadow's dad went out of his way to keep his youngest son naïve to the streets, Colt gave him enough rope to hang himself. Colt was of the thinking that Shadow's education in the streets would serve him just as well as the one he was receiving at the fancy private school his parents had him enrolled in—so he let him watch and learn, and Pain was one of his many street teachers.

Though Shadow and Pain were nearly the same age, Pain had always been more like a big brother. He had been on the streets since he was old enough to walk. His father had been a famous rapper who was murdered over a drug beef, and his mother a suicide victim. This left Pain's grandmother, Ms. Pearl, to raise him up. But Ms. Pearl was old enough that she couldn't really keep up with the wild young boy. Pain had been an outlaw in the truest sense, and soaked up everything he saw and heard from the older guys he hung around. It was these lessons that he passed on to Shadow.

As they grew older, however, they also started to grow apart. While Shadow was being groomed to be the savior of his family, Pain was becoming a menace in the streets. They didn't get to run together every day like they had when they were kids, but every chance Shadow got to sneak away from his family's suburban home, he would head straight to Brooklyn to hit the streets with Pain. No matter how much time passed between seeing each other, they would always pick up right where they left off.

"'Sup wit' you, Prince Charming?" Pain said.

"Feeling like the frog still waiting to get kissed." Shadow laughed.

"In time, baby boy . . . in time." Pain pulled his fingers free of Shadow's with a snap, then looked to Mussa, who was watching him from the stoop. "Peace, OG. What's the word?"

"Pain," Mussa said with a nod. "Or is it Blackbird now?"

"Blackbird?" Shadow looked to his friend.

"You didn't know? Your boy's been making quite a name for himself as the right hand to the queen of the Crows." Mussa looped his thumbs together and wiggled his fingers to mimic a bird flapping his wings. "Allah be merciful to those who fall under the shadow of the Blackbird, or so I hear."

"That's the problem with y'all old heads," Pain shot back. "You always taking gossip and running with it as gospel."

"And the problem with you young gangsters is that you *are* the problem," Mussa countered. "When are you brothers gonna learn that dealing in poison and death ain't doing nothing but speeding up the genocide of our people?"

"When you self-righteous old niggas stop talking *at* us and start talking *to* us," said Pain. "The day one of you street-corner preachers can provide us with a different way to put food in the bellies of these babies crying and dying from hunger is the day I'll hang up my pistols and walk a straight line. Until then, it's in your best interest to stay outta my mix."

Mussa's eyes darkened. "I ain't sure how I feel about how you're speaking to me, brother. Don't let this kufi fool you. Islam has made me a better man, but I'm still a man."

"I ain't your brother or your concern. You can preach that bullshit to Shadow until your lips fall off, but I'm cut different. I'm outside, old head, and can't you or nobody else send me back in the house."

"You sure about that?" Mussa said.

"Absolutely." Pain's right hand drifted to the pocket of his jacket.

Shadow watched the exchange between the two men, uncertain of what to do. Mussa saw Pain and men who moved like him as the roots of the problems plaguing inner-city communities, and Pain saw Mussa as one more ex-junkie looking down his nose at other people as soon as he got clean. This was an old argument between them, and they often traded barbs, but now things were getting too heated.

"Everybody just take a beat," Shadow finally said, stepping between them, facing Mussa with his back to Pain. There was a look in the older man's eyes that Shadow knew all too well: murder. "Mussa?"

Hearing Shadow call his name brought Mussa back from wherever his mind had traveled to. "Yeah, maybe we should," he said, but was still glaring at Pain. "I got an errand to deal with, Shadow, but think about what I said. Run it by your mom and see how she feels."

"I will, and thanks, Mussa."

"You really wanna thank me? Find yourself some safer friends to hang around with. Allah has a different path for you to walk, but the journey has to start with *you*." Mussa laid a hand on Shadow's shoulder again. Before leaving, he had some parting words for Pain: "I'm going to pray for you, brother."

"Give your prayers to my enemies," Pain said. "They're the ones who need them."

All Mussa could do was shake his head. He liked to think that every soul had the potential to be redeemed, no matter how dark—but with Pain, he wasn't so sure.

CHAPTER 7

"Why you had to come at Mussa like that?" Shadow asked Pain as the two of them sat on the stoop passing what was left of Shadow's joint back and forth.

"Fuck Mussa," Pain said, picking under his fingernail with a knife. "I ain't fooled by that holier-than-thou front he putting on. Drop an eight ball in his path and I'll bet it makes it right up his nose."

"You got Mussa wrong, man. He's a lot of things, but I can't see him backsliding." Shadow knew Mussa's story very well—how hard he had fought to get off drugs and change his ways. He'd put in too much work to return to this old lifestyle.

Pain peered at his friend. Shadow almost always saw the good in people, no matter how scurvy. He didn't have it in him to shatter Shadow's image of Mussa by revealing what he knew of the reformed drug addict's extracurricular activities. That wasn't his place. Shadow would have to see Mussa the way Pain knew him to be on his own time. "Bless you and your trusting heart. You're one of the last honorable niggas left, Shadow."

"Attribute it to me coming up around solid cats like yourself," Shadow said, then shifted gears. "What's with you and that damn Rambo knife? You're gonna fuck around and cut your finger off."

"You know I've been playing with blades since I was a little kid." Pain laid the knife flat on the back of his hand and plucked it, causing it to spin like a top, before flinging it into the air and catching it by the handle. "These things are second nature to me."

"You better stop those circus tricks before you hurt yourself."

"Or hurt somebody else." Pain retracted the blade into its grip and passed it to Shadow.

The handle was black and smooth, with grooves that made it easy to hold. Shadow hit the button on the side and the silver blade reappeared. "I can't lie, this knife is *cold*."

"A gift from my old head, War. It's saved my ass more times than I can count."

"I can imagine." Shadow hit the button again and the blade retracted. He started to pass it back, but Pain refused.

"You like it? Keep it. I got plenty more."

"Good looking out." Shadow slipped the knife into his pocket. "So, you running around with that biker gang after the queen's freak show almost killed you?"

"It's not a gang, it's a club," Pain said. "And you can bet your ass that was the first and last time Prophet will ever raise his hand against me . . . or what's left of it." He chuckled.

Prophet was the queen of the Crows's high executioner, a tattoo-covered albino with a reputation for being a ruthless killer. He had been in prison when Pain was first recruited by the Crows, a crew of thieves who were led by the outlaw queen Cassandra Savage. By the time Prophet was released and returned to take his rightful place by the queen's side, Pain had replaced him as her new favorite boy toy. This didn't sit well with Prophet and he never made a secret of it. Every chance he got, he went out of his way to slight the young upstart bandit. The bad blood between them eventually boiled over and resulted in violence. Prophet had nearly killed Pain, but in the battle, Shadow's best friend had hacked off two of the other man's fingers. He'd done it with the very same knife he had just gifted Shadow.

"So tell me something, P," Shadow said after a minute of silence. "What's that old-head pussy like?"

"C'mon, man."

"For real, dawg. Look, I've fucked older chicks before, but none of them on the level of old Queen Cass. That broad is not only fine as hell for her age, but about as ruthless as they come. The way she's always strutting around in those tight-ass leather pants, I know she's got some good pussy!"

"Is pussy all you ever think about?"

"What else is there?" Shadow said.

"Money, nigga!"

"That's something that I unfortunately don't know much about at the moment," Shadow said. "But I need to learn pretty damn quick." He filled Pain in on the conversation he'd had with Maureen that morning.

"Damn, shit must be critical if Madam Queen is trying to force her baby boy to put on the crown."

"Yeah, Mom's bugging." Shadow sighed.

"Is she?"

"So, you're saying you agree with her?"

"I don't know if I totally agree, but I don't disagree either. All the years I've known you and your family, all you've done is complain about your dad shutting you out of the real shit. Chance is locked up and Ghost is gone. By rights, it should be *you* wearing the crown, whether you want it or not. Not that fucking poseur who's calling the shots."

"It isn't that simple, Pain. Ghost and my dad had soldiers and respect in the streets. Even my Uncle Chapman has men loyal to him. What do *I* have?"

"The right!" Pain replied. "Do you think the streets respected Ghost because he was Chancellor King's son? Fuck no—he earned it. When your daddy pushed Ghost off the porch, he didn't wait around for the streets to respect him, he did what he had to do to ensure they had no choice. Now, I know you ain't the beast that Ghost was, or ruthless like your daddy, but you are the true-born heir."

"So I'm just supposed to go out in the streets with nothing but my name and my dick in my hand? We both know how that'll play out." Shadow could see it now: him running around with his chest poked out, talking about what's owed to him. He gave it a week before he'd end up dead.

"Shadow, you're one of the smartest dudes I know, but you ain't got a lot of common sense. Especially when it comes to street politics. You can't go about this like Ghost and try to take it, because that ain't in your nature. You're more like your dad. You've got to approach this like he did when he was running for office. Chance knew he could never win against them white folks by trying to *take* the office, so he convinced them to give it to him. Shadow, you walk in a light so bright that men like me are attracted to it like moths to a flame. Shine that light, and pull in the pieces you'll need close to you. You're looking at this like a war, instead of a campaign."

Shadow couldn't lie—Pain was making a whole lot of sense. More than his mother had. Maureen was a sweet lady, but a gorilla at heart, and that just wasn't Shadow's way. Pain had given him some food for thought, though he still had reservations. "Campaigns take money to fund, and that's something I don't have right now."

"And this is the part where you might have to get your hands a little dirty, sweet Prince. Your foundation will have to be built from the mud, so you gotta take it to the streets to get up the capital."

"What are you suggesting? That I fall in line with you and the Crows on some stickup shit?" Shadow made his fingers into a gun and started firing imaginary shots in the air.

"Hell nah! You're probably one of the worst thieves I ever met. Whenever we were boosting and got caught, it was always because *you* did some nut shit." When they were younger, Shadow would sometimes roll out with Pain and Fresh when they were on thievery missions in the mall. It wasn't because he needed the money; he just wanted to be included. "I got an idea where we might be able to get a little start-up product to get the ball rolling—but you might not like it."

PART II

DIRTY TRUTHS

CHAPTER 8

If Cindy Cunningham had to sum up her reaction when she stepped out of the subway station onto Canal Street that morning in one word, it would have been: *overwhelming!* She was a country girl, born and raised in Chubbuck, Idaho. In her twenty years on earth, the closest she'd ever come to a big city was when her dad had let her ride with him to Boise to get a replacement part for their old tractor that seemed to break down every other spring. She could remember marveling at the double-decker bus as it rumbled down Main Street—but New York's Chinatown at high noon was a whole different animal.

This was Cindy's third day in the city. The first two had been spent in a shoddy short-stay that her current boyfriend had procured for her somewhere out in Queens. She had met Charlie on an Internet dating site; he was handsome, with olive skin and a mop of black hair that Cindy had fantasized about long before she ever touched it in real time. He had reminded her of a young Ray Liotta when he played Henry Hill in *Goodfellas,* and she wanted nothing more than to be his Karen Hill. This was how, after only twenty days of virtual dating, Charlie was able to convince her to ride three days on a Greyhound to visit him in New York City so he could help her recognize her full potential.

Cindy had high expectations when she left Idaho, but so far the trip had been a disappointment. Charlie had promised to show her the town, but the only sights she had seen so far had been out the window of the grungy Queens apartment. It was just one room, with a leaking sink and a shared toilet in the hallway. To Charlie's credit, he had come to check in on her every day since she'd arrived, though he had only stayed long enough to feed her McDonald's and fuck her silly. He hadn't slept over, explaining that he was always on call for work. And he warned her that New York was too dangerous for a young woman to walk around alone. So she had suffered through this for two days. On the third morning, Cindy began to realize that she had made a mistake in running off to New York to visit Charlie.

She had started packing her things soon after waking up that day, planning to take the next bus back to Idaho, when Charlie showed up and told her to get dolled up—they were stepping out. He apologized for being so absent for the last few days, and blamed it on a big account that needed all his attention at work. Now that he had finally closed the deal, he wanted to celebrate with her and some of his coworkers at one of his favorite spots in Little Italy. Cindy's thoughts of going back home had immediately flown out the room's cracked window. Thirty minutes later, she was dressed in her best outfit and riding with Charlie on the subway into Manhattan.

"Miss . . . Miss . . . got some nice bags over here," said a tall, dark-skinned man. "Come check them out!"

Cindy had been attempting to take a selfie in front of one of the Chinese shops, and the man had stepped right into her shot. He was holding a green Hermès handbag.

"Wow, that's pretty." Cindy had only ever seen a Hermès on the Internet or while watching *The Kardashians*.

"And so are you," the man said. "It'll look good on you, pretty girl. And I'll give you a good price on it."

Cindy was about to take the bag from him for a closer look when Charlie stepped in.

"She don't want none of that bootleg shit you're out here peddling. Try that crap on one of these other tourists."

"I don't do bootleg," the man responded. "This is official merchandise."

"You got the paperwork that comes with it?" Charlie asked.

The tall man didn't answer.

"Exactly. Now take a walk before you find yourself packed up and shipped back to Africa in a box."

"Fuck you, I was born in Roosevelt Hospital."

"Just because you were born here don't make you an American. Now beat it, Chicken George."

"Asshole," the tall man mumbled, stalking off.

Charlie turned to Cindy. "What did I tell you about talking to strangers?"

"I wasn't talking to him," she said. "He was trying to sell me a bag."

"More like trying to fleece you. I keep telling you, doll, this ain't Idaho where it's cool to be all trusting. This is New York City and you gotta be ready to swim with the sharks or get eaten." He took her hand and nibbled her fingers playfully. "Now, let's go before you make me hurt somebody over you."

When Charlie had told Cindy they were going out to brunch in Little Italy, she'd had visions of a big restaurant with an exotic Italian name that she would struggle to pronounce. While there, she would stuff herself with pasta and listen to

Charlie and his coworkers exchange Mafia stories. So she had a hard time hiding her disappointment when they arrived at a small coffee shop on a narrow side street.

"Are we stopping here before going to the restaurant?" she asked.

"Who said anything about a restaurant? I told you we were gonna celebrate at my favorite place to eat. This is it!" Charlie waved his arm at the dusty green awning with the word *Bruno's* printed across it.

"C'mon, Charlie. You made me put on my good dress to go drink coffee?" Cindy folded her arms across her chest.

"Coffee? Kid, calling what Bruno does to a cup of joe simply *coffee* is an insult to the man's pedigree. These grounds come from home—none of that Colombian stuff is served here. And on top of that, they make the best chicken parmigiana in the city. Just trust me." He put his arm around her shoulders and escorted her toward the entrance.

There were two small, round tables outside of Bruno's for people who wanted to enjoy their coffee with fresh air. Only one of them was occupied at the moment. Three young men sat around it, sipping coffee and smoking cigarettes. Their conversation immediately trailed off, and three sets of eyes turned to the couple as they approached. Charlie was familiar with all three faces, but only one of them really mattered. At least in that neighborhood.

Dickey Salvatore sat in the middle with his back to the coffee shop, giving his dull green eyes a clear view of everything that moved on the street. His gaze hung on Charlie only briefly before turning to Cindy. He took one look at her off-the-rack dress and her sandals that exposed a big toe that had been hand-painted in a bedroom rather than a salon, and he already knew her story. He took a drag off the joint he'd been smoking and exhaled slowly. "If you're looking for IHOP, I think you're a few blocks off," he said.

Dickey wasn't trying to be funny, but his words nonetheless provoked laughter from the two goons sitting with him. Cindy's face went red and she turned to her companion, who looked just as uncomfortable.

"Take it easy, Dickey," said Charlie. "My girl's from out of town. It's her first time in the big city. I promised her I'd give her a taste of my home, so what better place to bring her than Bruno's?"

"If I was trying to impress a pretty young lady, I don't know if I'd bring her to this dump." This was Joe, aka "the Boot." They called him that because in the summer his skin got so deeply tanned that he could pass for a light-skinned Black guy. Only those who knew the Boot well were aware that his family was from the Old Country; he had roots that stretched as far back as the Roman emperors. "I'll bet he's been feeding you shit pizza and McDonald's since you've been here."

Charlie chuckled awkwardly—the Boot's comment had hit a little too close to home. "They've got a decent Chinese joint by the hotel too, but she ain't very picky." He was attempting to match the Boot's humor, but his words fell flat. "So, how's the chicken parm today? I've been bragging about it to my lady and can't wait for her to try it."

"Afraid that ain't possible—Bruno's is closed today," said Petey, the third man at the table. He was younger than the Boot and Dickey, but carried himself like a man wise beyond his years. He was someone who avoided trouble, while his counterparts were always out looking for it.

"What are you talking about?" Charlie responded. "It's eleven a.m. on a Thursday. I could set my watch by this place's hours of operation." He peered through the front glass and saw several people inside the establishment. His momentary confusion cleared right up when two black SUVs pulled over to the curb and the three seated men stood to attention.

Monster's Timberlands were the first to hit the sidewalk, followed by two dudes who'd been riding in the backseat. Monster stepped to the curb, tapping a fresh pack of Newports on the back of his knuckles before ripping the plastic off the top. His eyes did a quick sweep of the block, while he slid one of the cigarettes out and placed it between his blubbery lips. He ignored the three Italians who had stood to greet him and lumbered toward the second SUV, lighting his cigarette. He knocked twice on the hood, letting the passengers know that it was all clear. With near military precision, the driver and passenger doors of the second SUV opened simultaneously.

Two men spilled out, one tall and lanky with a face you were likely to forget shortly after seeing it, the other short, barely five seven, with a stocky build and thick, gangly arms. He was known as Lil Man because of his height, though when it was time for action, he carried himself like a giant. He was Monster's new protégé and, when necessary, personal attack dog. Once the two men were in position, Monster opened the back door of the SUV to reveal its precious cargo.

A woman stepped out first, with the help of Monster. He took one of her manicured hands in his and kept her steady while she placed the stilettos of her white thigh-high boots on the pavement. A white leather catsuit hugged her sleek frame, pushing up her forty-thousand-dollar breast implants. She looked like a rich porn star in her prime. This was Clarisse King, Monster's aunt and the only sister of the former king of Five Points. On the streets she was called Lady Snow, because of her skill at mixing drugs. Clarisse was a tall drink, standing close to six feet in flats, though she was rarely seen without heels. She liked for most men to have to look up at her when she was speaking. Clarisse was royalty, and it showed in the way she carried herself and how she handled business. Had it not been for gender, she could've very well been wearing the crown instead of Chance when their father handed it down.

The next person to exit the vehicle was Chapman King, Monster's uncle and Clarisse's fraternal twin. He was dressed in a white suit and pink shirt, with a lime-green tie. His processed hair was fried, dyed, and laid to the side with an old-school part. Chapman walked with a 1970s R&B vibe. He and Clarisse had been split from the same egg, but that was where their similarities ended. Chapman had always been everyone's least favorite of the four King siblings, which is why their father, Edward, had bestowed the crown on the younger Chancellor.

Their father's slight was something that Chapman would never forget, so he had bided his time waiting for the opportunity to usurp his little brother. After Chance was arrested and his true heir, Ghost, was murdered, Chapman stepped right over his nephew's grave to lay claim to something that had never been meant for him in the first place. He now wore the crown, though he hadn't earned it, which is why there were some who, behind closed doors, referred to him as a false king.

"I wasn't expecting such a large entourage for a friendly sit-down," Dickey greeted, shaking Chapman's hand.

"Just a few members of our inner circle," Chapman said. Meetings involving the Monarchy were usually limited to the king, his lords, and possibly an advisor or two. Chapman had rolled in with a small war party.

"Inner circle? If it wasn't for the pretty broad, we could've mistook you boys for the New York Knicks," the Boot joked, shooting his empty coffee cup into a nearby trash can like a basketball.

"Comments like that will get your jaw wired," Monster said. "I ain't my Uncle Chance or Ghost." He had never cared for Dickey or his crew—they were disrespectful. Chance had always let their smart remarks slide, but Monster was his own man.

Clarisse spoke up: "At least let me run a few drinks through my bladder before we get the pissing contest started." Her eyes were hidden behind large white sunglasses, though she was clearly watching everyone.

"He's just busting balls, Lady Snow," Dickey said with a smile. "Pay him no mind." He then turned his attention back to Chapman. "I'll walk you and your sister in, but the soldiers have to stay out here."

"I ain't just no soldier," Monster countered. "Where my uncle goes, I follow."

"So I keep hearing," Dickey said. "I'm still not sure if that's a good thing or a bad thing. In any event, we can discuss the finer points of regicide at another time. The Monarchy is waiting."

CHAPTER 9

The inside of Bruno's was just as drab as the outside. It was a small spot, barely big enough to fit the half-dozen tables. To the right of the entrance was the counter, with a glass display divided into two sections. One side was for pastries and the other for cold cuts. Normally, the dining area of Bruno's was filled with both tourists and locals, but that morning it was relatively empty. A handful of button men sat around at the tables, drinking coffee and killing time. These weren't soldiers like Lil Man, who was waiting outside, but they weren't part of the Monarchy either. They were "associates," ranking higher than common shooters but without having earned enough stripes to have seats at the big table. Two of them nodded in greeting at the passing king, but the others just stared.

Monster made eye contact with each and every one of them, holding that contact until they either averted their eyes or understood just what he was about. He wasn't trying to start anything, yet he knew how some of them felt about Uncle Chapman, and needed to let them know that the king hadn't rolled in with a sucker. Chapman might've been considered a bitch, but Monster was a stone-cold killer and wouldn't hesitate to show it. When Monster finally turned away from these men, he found Dickey watching him with a smirk.

Dickey led them through the dining area and down a narrow hallway to a wooden door. He paused with his hand on the knob, as if having second thoughts, then took another moment to smooth out his suit and straighten his tie before pushing the door open and revealing a larger dining room. This part of the coffee shop was rarely used, though Bruno would occasionally rent it out to those close to him for private parties.

Five men were sitting at the rectangular table, three on one side, two on the other, with a vacant space at the head. In chairs against the wall were their seconds-in-command. The men at the table ranged in age from their late thirties to their sixties, all coming from different walks of life. A casual observer might not have noticed anything special about them, but those in the know would immediately recognize them as the Monarchy: a collective of businessmen and gangsters assembled by Chancellor King. Each appointed lord of the Monarchy was powerful in his own territory, and collectively they controlled nearly every illegal operation south of Houston in Manhattan, along with various sections of Brooklyn and Queens. Nothing moved in those areas without the word of at least one of the five lords, and the Monarchy didn't move without its king.

Chairs scraped the floor as men at the table rose when Chapman entered the room. This was customary, a sign of respect. Four of the lords honored the tradition, yet there was one who remained seated: Rocco Salvatore, Dickey's father. Rocco was an old-school mobster, having become a made man when the oath still meant something. He sported a head of white hair, but had the physical build of a man half his age. Thick arms pressed against the seams of his salmon-colored suit jacket, and hands nearly the size of baseball mitts sat folded on the table. A cigar smoldered in an ashtray in front of him. He had the same dull green eyes as his son, only Rocco's were harder. They were the eyes of a man who had seen everything he needed to in this life, and was okay moving on to the next.

"Something wrong with your legs today, Mr. Salvatore?" Clarisse addressed the elephant in the room.

Rocco took a puff of his cigar, then slowly expelled the smoke and savored the flavor for a moment before responding. "It's not my legs that are keeping me in this chair. It's my gout." He motioned toward his left foot. "They call it the 'disease of kings.' You familiar?" The question was directed at Chapman, who didn't answer. "Don't suppose you have. When it flares, it makes it a painful task to walk, let alone stand. Even if it's to show respect to our new king. No offense."

Clarisse started to say something, but Chapman beat her to it: "None taken, Rocco. Who amongst us would not make exceptions to antiquated rules for the sake of our elders? After all, it was the seeds men like you planted that made it possible for these trees to grow." He glanced around the room, purposely skipping over the lords of the Monarchy, instead acknowledging their seconds-in-command. Chapman walked to the head of the table and positioned himself in front of the vacant chair, then paused dramatically before sitting down. Monster pulled up two chairs and set them on either side of his uncle, then offered Clarisse a seat in one of them and took the other for himself. Chapman wiggled around in his chair for a few beats as if trying to get comfortable before motioning to the four standing lords that they could retake their seats.

"Nice of you to join us," muttered Billy Wong, a handsome Chinese man with wavy black hair and thin lips. He and his brother Max were heroin importers and had been doing business in Five Points for two generations.

"My apologies for being so tardy," Chapman said, "but traffic is always a bitch getting into this part of the city, no matter how early you start out. Maybe we should think about moving where we hold court. I know a few spots in Midtown that would be happy to accommodate us."

"Five Points business being handled in Midtown feels like an oxymoron to me," said Henry Atume, a Nigerian man who appeared to be in his late thirties, and the only other Black man at the table. Henry had come to the United States on a student visa when he was eighteen, and spent his first year and a half starving in New York City while trying to keep up with his studies. This changed when he met a female friend from back home who showed him a way to make more money in six months than he could make in five years with a college degree. They started out with CDs and DVDs, and when the Internet revolution kicked in, Henry switched hustles. He and his crew now controlled the vast majority of the knockoff trade in Five Points. They could bootleg anything from bags to shoes to watches and beyond. Henry and his boys brought in a great deal of money to the Monarchy, so it gave him a louder voice than some of the others at the table.

"You act like this is Castle Grayskull and the magic can only come from here," Chapman said with a chuckle, referencing the *He-Man* cartoon. "Where we make our decisions isn't as important as *what* decisions we make. We can stand on business anywhere. Why not at least do it someplace more befitting men of our stature?" He looked to Bruno. "No offense."

"I'm bigger on tradition than ambiance—it's tradition that keeps everybody honest," remarked Lito Garcia, a sharply dressed man of about forty, and the only Hispanic at the table. Lito was the Monarchy's biggest earner. His business was cars—stealing them and chopping them up for resale. His specialty were the exotic vehicles that his crew snatched off the streets, which were usually resold in Europe. Had it not been for Chapman snatching the throne when his brother and nephew fell, Lito might've been granted the crown.

"Honesty in a room full of criminals?" Monster spoke up. "I doubt it, but I see your point." All eyes turned to him.

The king's court was generally exclusive to the Council of Lords and their immediate seconds, other than occasional instances where an outsider was brought in to address business that pertained to the full Monarchy. Monster had been Chapman's coconspirator in the plot to grab the throne, and had by default become the new king's right-hand man. Chapman had promised him all the perks that came with his new position, though his uncle's word wasn't good enough. Monster had demanded to be brought before the court to make it official. Chapman had reluctantly agreed; he needed Monster and his soldiers—at least for the moment.

"For those of you who aren't familiar," said Chapman, "this is my nephew Monster. My dear departed Colt's son."

"I knew your dad," Billy Wong said. "Handled some business for my family a few years back. Very, very efficient man."

Not long before Colt's death, Chance had put him and the Reapers on loan to the Wong family to handle a dispute they were having with some Korean hoods who had been encroaching on their territory. The Wongs had only wanted the Reapers to scare them, but Colt King didn't do fear. He did death, which is what he administered to each and every member of the Korean gang. He even whacked a few of their civilian relatives to make sure he got his point across.

"No one could ever fill my brother's shoes, but Monster

has his . . . skills," Chapman explained. "This is why I have named him my second. Who better to guard my flank than my nephew?"

"I hope he does a better job watching your back than he did with Ghost," said Henry Atume. He had done a lot of business with Ghost, and Monster was always there shadowing him. He had liked Ghost, but never really cared for Monster.

"I'm sure my nephew's learned from his previous mistakes," said Chapman. "But that's my concern, not yours. Let's get to the business of what's brought us here."

"What's brought us here is the shipment of auto parts that my guys were supposed to pick up being seized at Port Newark," said Lito. "Those parts were to go on some cars scheduled to be shipped to Belize in four days. Without them, I can't make good on my delivery."

Chapman weighed the man's statement. "I can see how this little snag can present an inconvenience to you and your business."

"Inconvenience? I stand to lose close to half a million dollars if I don't carry out this shipment. I'd call that more than a fucking *inconvenience*."

"Relax, my friend," said Chapman. "This is an easy fix. Call your buyers and tell them that something's happened out of your control and the shipment will be delayed a few days. I'll make some calls and we'll get this sorted out. And as a show of good faith on the part of your new king, I'll even provide you some financial relief for your troubles. Fifty thousand should ease some of your pain. How does that sound?"

"Sounds like you're pissing on my head and trying to convince me that it's raining!" Lito slapped the tabletop. "This isn't just about the money, it's my reputation on the line here. When I give my buyers a date, that shit is etched in stone. I pride myself on doing what I say I'm going to do, which I understand might be a new concept to you, Your Highness."

"Let's mind our manners here," Clarisse growled.

"It's fine, sister," Chapman said, then turned to Lito. "That's a hell of a financial hit that you stand to take, so I'll overlook your little outburst. The real of it is this: we are all in businesses where we have to expect the unexpected. Your shipment got pinched, and I get it, but with the ports it's always a roll of the dice getting goods in and out. These things happen."

"Not under Chancellor they didn't," said Carmine Lupenza. He was the oldest person at the table, a balding man wearing a cheap suit and wire-rimmed glasses. He looked more like a bookkeeper than what he really was: underboss to one of the smaller Mafia families in the city and a retired contract killer. "With all due respect, Chapman, your brother put certain systems in place that prevented us from running into this kind of *snag*, as you called it. We were afforded certain comfortabilities because of his political ties. Ties which you assured us would remain intact when you petitioned to take your brother's vacant seat at this table, which we allowed."

"*Allowed?*" scoffed Chapman. "Need I remind you of one of this Monarchy's oldest traditions? For as long as this line survives, there will always be a King seated at the head of this table. Am I not the blood of my father? The crown is mine by right of birth!"

"More like by *default*," Lito shot back. "Had Ghost not been murdered right after his dad got locked up, I doubt we'd be having this conversation."

"Just what are you trying to say?" Clarisse snapped.

"Only what everyone here is probably thinking. The three men who stood between you and your daddy's crown all met with questionable ends." Colt and Ghost had been murdered, and Chance was staring at the prospect of years in prison.

"Are you suggesting that I would ever move against my own family?" Chapman said.

Lito let the question linger for a moment. "Of course not, my king. Only that you are one of the luckiest sons of bitches I've ever met."

"Now, now, let's not let this escalate into something it doesn't have to be," Rocco cut in. "It's no secret that I'm biased in this little family dispute. Chancellor is one of my oldest friends, and your nephew Ghost was like one of my own. It broke my heart to hear what happened to him. I think I speak for most of us gathered here when I say that the news of what happened to your brother and nephew rocked this table to the core. Chance was no stranger to the game, so he understood the rules. Even with his case looking dire, he's still alive to fight it. But Ghost . . . he didn't deserve to go out the way he did. I wanted justice for my friend. I wanted my pound of flesh from the men who gunned that poor boy down and left him to die like a dog in the street. And with respect to the Monarchy, the head of some patsy who may or may not have had a hand in it wasn't enough to slake my thirst for revenge." Rocco's eyes burned into Monster. "Alas," he continued, his tone softening as he looked around the table, "we came to a decision that the majority of us felt best served the Monarchy. This thing of ours is bigger than the personal feelings of one man. So, regardless of the circumstances under which the crown found its way to your head, Chapman, you are now king of Five Points—a decision made by this table and one that every man here will honor." He fixed his gaze on Lito.

"Which brings us back to the original point I believe Lito was trying to make," Carmine picked up. "When you . . .

succeeded your brother, assurances were made to this table. We would honor your claim so long as our businesses were not affected. This has not been the case."

"Do you mean to say that you're willing to let one seized shipment of auto parts call my leadership into question?" Chapman responded. "This is total bullshit!"

"If only this were just about the shipment," Billy said. "There's also the matter of all the bodies dropping in the streets over this civil war that's broken out within the King family. There's a lot of heat on you boys right now. Heat that we're all starting to feel."

"A few minor skirmishes by some upstart gangsters trying to lay claim to what doesn't belong to them," said Chapman. "Nothing more. They'll learn the folly of their actions soon enough."

"Then it's best we bring this meeting to a close," said Rocco, "so you can get to the business of teaching them."

Chapman paused as he tried to figure out if Rocco had just dismissed him. When he felt like enough time had passed so that he could leave without looking like a chump, he stood up from the table. "If there's nothing else, this meeting has come to an end."

Everyone else in the room stood as well, even Rocco, with Dickey's help. Chapman turned on his heels and left the room, followed by Clarisse.

Monster, however, stayed behind. His off-center eyes swept over each lord of the Monarchy, lips twisted into a smirk. "Y'all enjoy your fifteen minutes," he capped before slipping out of the room.

"I don't know who I like less, the uncle or the nephew," Henry said after the royal entourage had departed.

"Be careful, that's your king you're talking about," Dickey said with a scowl.

"He might wear the crown, but he ain't my fucking king," Lito said. "All he's done is make a fucking mess since he took the chair. I know I'm not the only one who's been actually losing money under his reign." He looked around at the other lords.

"Admittedly, I've been hearing some rumblings from our people as well," Dickey said. "But nothing too major. I attribute it to growing pains. Chapman is just getting used to his new position, that's all."

"Since when did you become such an advocate for Chapman King?" Lito rasped. "Your tongue used to cut the sharpest when it came to anything concerning that family, even when Chance was still at the head of the table."

Dickey shrugged. "I'm just trying to go with the flow so I can keep earning. Besides, it was you guys who crowned him. I don't have an official vote at this table, at least not yet." He laid his hand on Rocco's shoulder.

"You're right," Carmine said, "you don't have a say at this table—but you've been awfully opinionated since the changing of the guard. Yet your father, the head of your family, hasn't said too much." He turned to Rocco. "Your thoughts?"

The old man took a toke from his cigar before answering. "What does the opinion of a man who has one foot in and one foot out matter at this point? I'm halfway to retirement, so I don't see how my thoughts will carry any real weight as far of the future of this table goes. And as my son has already said, it was the decision of this Monarchy to place the crown on the head of that . . . man."

"Because he was the only game in town," Henry said.

"Was he?" Rocco replied, expelling a large cloud of smoke.

He let the question hang in the air for a time before raising the next topic with the Council of Lords.

CHAPTER 10

"I don't know if you are aware of this or not," Monster said over his shoulder to his uncle, "but you got the makings of a problem brewing." After leaving the court, Monster had switched from the SUV he'd arrived in and was now riding shotgun with Chapman and Clarisse. He had some things to discuss that weren't for the ears of the soldiers.

"Lito is upset about his shipment, so he was talking out of his ass," Chapman said. "He's strong on the streets, but not as strong as the Monarchy, and he'd be a fool to make a move against his king. It'll blow over."

"Fuck Lito!" Monster barked. "I'd rinse my gun in his mouth if he ever moved against this family. But it ain't only Lito I'm talking about. Or was I the only one who noticed how much the temperature had dropped by the time we left that room?"

"There was a point when I thought I might need a sweater," Clarisse said.

"Paranoia from Monster is to be expected, but you, Sis?" Chapman shook his head. "I hope them sour-ass old heads ain't got you second-guessing."

"Chapman, outside of Chance, you know I'm the only one in this world who would make something bleed on your behalf, with no questions asked," Clarisse said. "Don't ever forget that. I'm not concerned about what was said in that room. It's what *wasn't* said that has me feeling like we need to tighten up."

"So, what, you questioning my qualifications as king now?"

"Being that I was unfortunate enough to not be born with a dick, my opinion about however you decide to conduct Monarchy business will never really count for anything. But as long as one of my brothers sits on this throne, I will always do my best to protect the King interests."

"And what are *your* interests, Sister dear?"

"Making sure you don't fuck this up and get us all killed. Bullshit aside, we're all coconspirators in this, so I don't feel like we need to mince words. The move our little brother was about to make threatened the King legacy, so we did what we had to do, not just to ensure the future of this family, but our individual legacies as well. You sliding onto the throne was supposed to be a quiet transition, and you're making far too much noise. Our claim to the crown was shaky at best, and your attitude toward your new position isn't helping to steady it." Though she and Chapman were twins, split from the same embryo, she was the one who had inherited their father's survival instinct. Clarisse was good at reading rooms and body language, and what she had seen at the meeting gave her concern.

"And you've said all that to say *what*?" Chapman was starting to regret his decision to bring his sister along to Bruno's.

"She's saying that you need to take your boots off the table and put them on the ground," Monster cut in. "The key to Uncle Chance's reign was that he didn't just rule the people, he was *of* the people. Soldiers respect deeds, not words."

"And as I've already stated, I'm not my brother."

"Obviously," Clarisse said under her breath.

Chapman shot her a dirty look. "Mutineers . . . I'm surrounded by mutineers!" He threw up his hands. "I don't even know why it matters so much to the two of you to appease the old guard, when the plan is to bring in a new one."

"Because all that we've sacrificed will have been for nothing if your arrogant ass gets overthrown before you've even had a chance to get comfortable on the throne," Clarisse countered. "Get your head out of your ass and in the game."

"Fine. If me taking a more hands-on approach will make you two crybabies feel better, that's what I'll do. Starting with the meeting later tonight."

"That won't be necessary, Unc. Me and Judah got that under control." Monster's words edged on panic.

"Oh, I'm sure you're a more-than-capable liaison, Nephew, but as you pointed out, our soldiers respect deeds and not words. What better way to prove my commitment to the cause than to stand with you on the front lines when we solidify things with our new allies? Unless, of course, there's a reason you don't want me at this meeting?"

"No, it's nothing like that. I just figure that with your profile as high as it is right now, we don't want to run the risk of you being spotted amongst a group of known criminals."

"Now, is that any way to speak about the men who're going to help us make our hold over this city absolute?" Chapman gave Monster a playful look. "As thoughtful as it is for you to have my best interests at heart, this is a risk I'm more than willing to take, considering what's at stake. If the old Monarchy is to be burned down and we're going to build a new one from its ashes, it's only fitting that it's the king who lights the match. Unless either of you have a problem with this . . ." He turned to his sister.

"I think it's a bad idea," Clarisse said, "but like the Burger King slogan goes, have it your way."

Chapman now looked to Monster, whose jaw was flexing under the keloid scar on his cheek. He had something to add, but swallowed it and simply said, "You're the king."

Chapman smiled like a snake who'd just caught a field mouse sleeping. "Indeed I am, and the both of you had better damn well remember it."

CHAPTER 11

After the second meeting at Bruno's that took place following the departure of the Kings, the lords of Five Points dispersed back to their respective domains. Rocco and Dickey Salvatore were the last to leave the establishment. Rocco had insisted on getting some coffee and a few pastries to go, then let Dickey lead him out into the afternoon sun.

"Your gout giving you trouble?" Dickey asked, noticing his dad's slight limp. He reached his hand out to take his father's arm, but the elder Salvatore waved him off.

"Nothing more than annoyance. I'll be fine." Rocco's left foot was indeed causing him pain, but he had always been a proud man and liked to do things on his own. Help was for the weak.

Rocco's Lincoln Continental idled at the curb. Leaning against it and talking shit with the soldiers was a man named Vincent Apora who was not quite as old as Rocco, but not too far behind either. In his prime, Vincent had been a hit man for the Salvatore family, but these days he acted as more of a companion and bodyguard to Rocco. When he noticed the mob boss and his son approaching, Vincent dismissed the soldiers and opened the back door for Rocco. Dickey motioned for him to give them a second. There was something he needed to discuss with his old man.

"Pop, were you serious about that stuff you were saying in there?"

"Don't read too deep into it, Son. The Council of Lords is faced with a problem and I offered them some possible solutions. Whether they actually take them into consideration or not will be for them to decide. I'm an old man who'll soon be retired, and as I've said, my voice doesn't carry the weight it once did."

"I call bullshit. You can play the feeble-old-man role with the Monarchy, but you and I both know your grip on those puppet strings is just as firm as it's ever been. You just took a baseball bat to a hornets' nest in there, so don't act like it was just nothing. Be honest with me. I'm your son."

"Yes, blood of my blood and flesh of my flesh." Rocco stroked his son's ear like he had when Dickey was a kid. "You are my greatest joy . . . and my greatest disappointment." He twisted Dickey's ear until the young man yelped in pain. "You want honesty? Then let me give you some. There's a difference between being old and being a fool, which is what you've been taking me for in all of this."

"Pop, what the hell are you talking about?"

"Don't play me, you little weasel. You think I didn't notice the sideways glances between you and that freak show Monster? Or how all of a sudden you've thrown your support behind someone who we both know you don't respect?"

"I'm just trying to do what's best for the Monarchy!" Dickey said.

"More like trying to do what's best for *you*." Salvatore released Dickey, who took a cautious step back, rubbing his bruised ear.

"Pop, I don't know what you think you know, but—"

"What I think and what I know are two different things. I've always known you to be ambitious, sometimes to your detriment, but I've never thought you'd be stupid enough to tie a noose around your own neck. You know that's what you've done, right? By helping Monster and his Uncle Chapman in their little uprising, you've hung yourself, my boy."

It wasn't *what* Rocco said that sent icy pinpricks through Dickey's chest, it was *how* he'd said it. Even if Dickey wanted to deny it, he couldn't. His father knew him too well not to recognize his fingerprints on this. Dickey had figured it would come out eventually, but not before he'd had a chance to make his next move.

After an uncomfortable silence, the younger man found his voice: "You all agreed that Chancellor King handing the reigns to Ghost while he played politician was bad for the Monarchy. That was you in the room with the other old-timers when you all came to this conclusion, right?"

Rocco raised his hand as if about to take a swing. "Don't get fucking cute with me. I'll give you a good slap is what I'll do." After a few moments had passed, he lowered his hand and regained his composure. "You even knowing this means that you've been ear-hustling—but not paying attention. I could give two shits about who sits at the head of that table. God bless the poor bastard wearing the crown and all the heat that'll come with it, so long as it doesn't affect our family's income. Chancellor King's connections put us in rooms we wouldn't otherwise be in, and handing the crown to Ghost would've cast us back to the Dark Ages."

"Then what's the big deal about changing the pecking order? If anything, you and the entire Monarchy should be thanking me for having the nuts to do what none of you seemed to be willing to do, and that's salvaging our future. You needed a king and I gave you a puppet whose strings we can pull anytime we feel like it, Pop. You should be celebrating me, not judging me."

"Celebrate you for what? Crossing a friend of ours into prison and murdering his oldest son?"

"But you said—"

"Me saying that I didn't agree with what Chance was about to do wasn't the same as me wanting to send him to prison or have his son murdered and then replaced with that idiot brother of his. Chapman lacks not only the connections Chance had, but also the respect. Chance had his hang-ups, yet no one can deny that he was well respected, which is why he made such an efficient king. Chapman couldn't hold his brother's dick while he pissed and not splash it everywhere. He's a natural fuckup. That isn't an insult, it's a fact."

"Then why give him the crown?"

"Because overly ambitious little upstarts such as you and Monster didn't leave us a choice. The timing of Chance getting pinched and Ghost getting murdered right after that raised some uncomfortable questions. No matter how slick you lot thought you were, it was too big of a coincidence for people to ignore. Had anyone but Chapman put that crown on his head, it would've only reinforced the whisperings about the Kings having been betrayed, and fingers would've started getting pointed. Maybe even at us, thanks to you and your scheming. Do you realize what could happen if anyone even *suspected* that the Salvatores played a role in usurping a sitting king?"

"If its blowback you're worried about, don't," said Dickey. "All I did was pull a few strings. It was Monster and his crew that handled the ugly business—killing the kid and all."

"Which just makes it worse. Even if you didn't have a direct hand in Ghost's death, by participating in this clusterfuck of an overthrow, you've given that gorilla Monster and his pansy un-cle an axe to hold over your neck. And you'd be a fool to think they won't use it to cut your head clean off if it suits them. If a Salvatore had *truly* been behind this, there wouldn't be so many loose ends."

"What loose ends?" Dickey said. "Ghost is dead and Mon-ster is in our pocket. The Kings are done!"

This made Rocco laugh. "You sound so sure of yourself, and this tells me that even though you're in the game now, you're still not seeing the entire field, Son. In your haste to yank out the King family's fangs, you've neglected their claws."

CHAPTER 12

I t was late afternoon by the time Mike Porter arrived at his parents' house in Ridgefield Park, New Jersey. The drive from his apartment in Hempstead, Long Island, usually took about an hour, but that morning it had taken him closer to two because of the heavy traffic. He had an important meeting in the city that evening, and playing errand boy for his mother threatened to make him late. But what could he do? What Mother wanted, Mother got. That's how it had always been since he'd become a member of the little family.

Grace had called him that morning and asked that he swing by the house to grab some papers that the carrier of his dad's life insurance policy had requested. He'd thought about suggesting that his mother get the papers herself or send his brother Tom, since they were both in Manhattan, which was significantly closer to Ridgefield Park, but decided not to waste his breath. Tom's spoiled ass wasn't worth the sperm it took to create him. He was a lazy bastard and would likely spend the rest of his days leeching from the family. Getting him to do anything other than club hop and shove blow up his nose was like pulling teeth. His mother's reluctance to go to the house in

Jersey was a bit more understandable. She hadn't set foot in the mini mansion since the night her husband had been murdered there.

Mike's father had been a bigwig in the city. Alderman James Porter came from a family of politicians, so he had been groomed from an early age and his star rose quickly. In recent times, he had been positioning himself to make a run at the mayor's office, and early polls had been encouraging. From there, the sky would've surely been the limit—and there was no telling how far up the ladder he could have climbed.

Mike could still remember the night he had gotten the call from his mother. She was so hysterical that he couldn't understand what she was saying at first. She had just returned home from her monthly book club meeting when she made the discovery. Her husband had been viciously beaten and strangled. The detectives assigned to investigate the murder were calling it a "crime of passion," and Mike didn't disagree. Most killers opted for a gun, or even a knife, but his father's murderer had used their bare hands.

The news of Alderman Porter's death had sent shock waves through the city. There was an even greater uproar when the police made an arrest for the crime: Councilman Chancellor King. Chancellor and the alderman had never been close, but they had scratched each other's backs a time or two. Word was that Chance had had his eyes on the mayor's office as well, and that Porter was standing in his way so he'd had the alderman killed. Mike was acquainted with Chance through his own relationship with Lolli King, so he knew that wasn't the retired gangster's style. The story of Chance ordering the hit was a reach, especially considering the man's increasingly visible public profile, though his history of ties to the streets made it easier for the public to accept. In the end, several key parties had been satisfied: the police were finally able to bring down a man who had seemed untouchable for decades, and the Porter family had gotten justice.

Most men in Mike's position would've been thrilled at the life they'd been afforded, but then again, many people didn't understand the cost that came with being a part of such an affluent family. Granted, Mike benefited from the same luxuries as his half siblings—including a top-notch education and growing up in a large house—though the material rewards were where the comfort stopped. Mike was a true-born son of Alderman Porter, but had always been relegated to the background—like a shadow dancing on the fringes of the family light, yet never invited to stand in the glow with them. Sure, there were pictures of him sprinkled throughout the house with the rest of the family, but he could challenge anyone to find one of those images in public. When the Porters were on the campaign trail smiling for the cameras, they made sure to keep his Black ass out of the spotlight. For all the love they showed him behind closed doors, the shame of his existence always trumped that devotion in public.

Mike punched in the code on the front door and the device beeped twice before flashing a green light and unlocking. As he stepped inside, he was greeted by an eerie silence. In the past, the house would have been bustling at that time of day, with the staff going about their daily chores while Gretchen, their German chef, rattled plates in the kitchen as she got started on dinner.

From the foyer, Mike entered their spacious living room. His mother would've had a fit if she'd seen him stepping onto their white carpet in his sneakers, but she wasn't there to complain. His eyes went to the wall above the fireplace where a familiar portrait was mounted. There were his parents, his brother

Tom, his sister Lucy, and the little twins, Cam and Candice. Dressed in matching sweaters and smiling, they looked like the all-American family. But that changed with Mike in the picture: the lone brown spot on the perfect white portrait.

Mike had been adopted, or at least that was the story they told the media and the rest of the family when the little boy came to live with them. It was a lie that Mike wouldn't uncover until he was a little older—though it hadn't been a completely false narrative. Alderman Porter was in reality Mike's biological father, but Grace hadn't been his birth mother. The boy had been the product of an extramarital affair that Alderman Porter had been carrying on for years with one of his aids. When Mike was born, Alderman Porter had denied fathering the mixed-race child, yet the DNA results said otherwise. It would've made for quite the scandal had it ever gotten out, but the Porters had paid Mike's mother handsomely to disappear. A few years later, the woman was shot and killed during a home invasion, which left young Mike alone in the world.

Mike spent the next year bouncing around the foster care system, and would've likely remained there had it been left to Alderman Porter. He wanted nothing to do with the boy, and it was Grace who forced his change of heart. At the time, Lucy was an only child, and according to the doctors, Grace would never be able to have another baby of her own. She wanted desperately to give her husband a son, so she began considering adoption. When Grace suggested that they take in the son of her husband's deceased mistress, the alderman thought she had flipped her lid. This wasn't a decision that Grace had made easily, but it struck her as the right thing to do. Mike was just a kid and shouldn't be forced into a life of poverty when his biological father had so much to give. Mike might not have come from Grace's womb, but he was still a Porter. It took Grace threatening to leave with Lucy and expose the whole thing publicly before Alderman Porter reluctantly agreed. He pulled a few strings and Mike became a legal member of their family.

Years later, Grace would be blessed against all odds and became pregnant with Tom. Then blessed twice more with the twins. Growing up as one of the Porter kids, Mike was afforded everything that a child could dream of, except the love of his father. Grace, however, didn't treat him any different than the other kids. She loved him as much as she could, considering the circumstances, though Alderman Porter acted for the most part as if Mike didn't exist. On the rare occasion when he did acknowledge his bastard, it was to berate him or point out where he was falling short.

It wasn't until years later that Mike had learned the truth of how he came to live with them. Reflecting back, he had a totally different level of respect for Grace. He could only imagine how much of her dignity was stripped away every time she looked into his eyes and told him that she loved him—he must have been a constant reminder of her husband's infidelity.

Mike started to make his way upstairs to the filing cabinet in the closet of his parents' bedroom where Grace kept a lot of their important family documents. His foot had just touched the second step when he heard a faint noise, a low, rhythmic hum. It sounded like an air conditioner, but Mike had checked the house carefully the last time he was here and knew he hadn't left anything running.

There was someone else in the house.

Mike pulled his gun from the holster clipped to the back of his pants and crept quietly back through the living room. He checked the doors that led to the patio and found them locked. Same with the back door off the kitchen that the staff used to come and go. He was about to dismiss the noise as simply his imagination, when he heard it again. As he moved from the kitchen down the hall toward his father's office, he saw that the door was slightly ajar. A door that had definitely been closed when he left the house last time.

Gun at the ready, Mike peeked inside the office and glimpsed a figure dressed in black with a hood pulled over their head. The intruder's back was to him, looking down at a slip of paper. The person was so engrossed that they didn't hear Mike entering the room.

"Show me your hands or I'll show you your brains!" Mike shouted.

Startled, the intruder froze and slowly raised their hands, still holding the piece of paper.

"I don't know who you are, but you picked the wrong house to rob." Mike approached with his gun trained on the intruder's head.

The intruder moved so fast that Mike didn't even see it coming. A paperweight flew at Mike like a fastball. Thankfully, the weight only nicked the side of Mike's head—if it had connected squarely, it would've hurt him badly. Mike was disoriented and the figure made a second move, a spinning backkick that hit him right in the jaw. Pain exploded through his face. Mike tried to swing the gun around, but the intruder blocked his arm, causing the gun to go off, sending a bullet into the far wall. This was immediately followed by a knee to Mike's gut, knocking the wind out of him.

The intruder could fight, but so could Mike. He played possum and lured them closer. When the intruder was right on top of him, about to deliver another blow, Mike's fist shot up and slammed into their chin, sending them flailing backward and crashing onto the desk. Mike didn't give them a chance to get up—he grabbed them by a leg, sweeping them off the desk and onto the floor. Mike straddled the figure and pointed his gun at their face, ready to end their life. It was then that the hood fell away.

"Lollipop?" he gasped, recognizing the face of his occasional lover. "What the hell are you doing here?" Before she could response, the crumpled piece of paper she had been looking at caught his eye on the ground next to them. He knew immediately what she was doing there. "Lolli, I understand what this looks like, but I can explain. I was—"

Something heavy slammed into the back of his head and he lost consciousness.

CHAPTER 13

"Stupid, reckless girl! I told you this was a bad idea!" Nefertiti scolded once she and Lolli were back in her truck and away from the house. Nefertiti was behind the wheel, dressed in black jeans and a hoodie that was pulled slightly back from her head, showing off her beautiful onyx face. She had abandoned her usual black suit and white shirt for the day, dressing similar to Lolli to undertake the task she had been reluctantly talked into. Nefertiti was Lolli's bodyguard and shadow. Wherever the princess of the King family went, Nefertiti followed.

"That house has been sitting empty for I don't know how long," Lolli said. "How was I supposed to know somebody was gonna pop up? And besides, you were on lookout duty and you let him slip past. You should've warned me." She pulled open the center console, where several nip-sized bottles of Jack Daniel's were stored. She plucked two, downing one and then sipping the other.

"I *did*!" Nefertiti shot back. "Why do you think I was texting you?"

"Well, I didn't see any text. Maybe that bum-ass android

you refuse to get rid of didn't send it." Lolli sucked her teeth, then finished the nip and reached for a third one. Before she could grab it, Nefertiti slammed the compartment closed, almost taking off one of Lolli's fingers.

"Or maybe your ass was too faded to notice it. Lolli, you need to slow down. It's barely past noon and your ass is already half-drunk."

"Ain't nobody drunk. I just needed a little something to take off the edge after what just happened."

"That's the exact same thing you said when you took a shot before going into the house."

"Bitch, why you on my back? You ain't my mama!"

"You're right, because if you *were* my child, I wouldn't be just sitting here watching you try and drink your pain away."

"Fuck you!" Lolli snatched the compartment back open and grabbed another nip. She turned her head and stared out the window so Nefertiti couldn't see how deep the words had cut her. The truth was always painful.

Nefertiti held her tongue. She hadn't meant to come off so harsh, but it needed to be said. Lolli was spiraling and it seemed like Nefertiti was the only one with the balls to check her over it. Lolli was a girl who loved a good time, yet since the arrest of her father and the murder of her brother, she had been drinking a lot heavier. This was due in part to feeling like everything that had happened was her fault. And to an extent, it was. It had been her actions that sent the dominoes falling.

Chance had been planning to run for the office of Brooklyn borough president. To do that, he needed political allies, and few held as much sway in the key neighborhoods of Kings County as Alderman James Porter. Chance had been trying to recruit Porter to his cause, but the man was being difficult about it. Lolli couldn't understand why, because as far as she knew, the Porters and the Kings had traded favors since back when her grandfather was still running things. She had only been trying to help her father out when she paid an unannounced call on Alderman Porter, showing up at his home in the middle of a kid's party that they were hosting. Lolli wanted to talk to him and see if they could come to some type of understanding, so she had shown up with her hand extended in friendship, only to have Alderman Porter spit in it. He had dismissed her and her family like common ghetto trash, and had refused to help Chancellor in his push. He had told Lolli flat out that he planned to use his influence to *derail* Chancellor's run. Alderman Porter saw Chancellor King as a potential threat to his own run for mayor.

Lolli had left the Porter house feeling like the help, and that didn't sit well with her. She wasn't used to being denied, especially when it came to something that could help her family. So she had paid Alderman Porter a second visit. This time, instead of showing up with an open hand, she arrived with a closed fist. Lolli had worked Alderman Porter over for the better part of an hour, but to his credit, the tough old bastard never budged from his stance. In fact, he had doubled down—and now, instead of Chancellor being someone Alderman Porter simply didn't care for, he had become an enemy. Lolli had turned the situation from bad to worse. It had crossed her mind to take the alderman's life, but killing him right then and there would've been impulsive, and that wasn't Lolli's style. Everything she did had to be thought out and calculated. Besides, with someone as high-profile as Alderman Porter, there was no way she could've taken him out on the fly and gotten away with it.

So rather than killing him, she had taken her chances and let him live, then prayed that her rash decision wouldn't bring too much heat on the family. Little did she know, the heat that followed would soon burn everything down: someone else visited the Porter house soon after she'd left and had killed the alderman, hanging the crime on her father. Lolli was determined not to rest until she found out who had done this, and why. Which is what had led her back to the scene of the crime today.

"Let me address the real elephant in the room, though," Nefertiti said after several minutes of silence. "What the fuck was Mike doing there? That boy has been in the streets for as long as we've known him. Why would he be coming to Alderman Porter's house? Better question: who gave him their security code to get through the front door? Something doesn't smell right, Lolli."

"Yeah, I smell it too." Lolli looked down at the receipt she had picked up after her scuffle with Mike. She had read it five times since she found it, hoping that she was reading it wrong.

"Did you at least find anything useful in there before I had to come in and save you?" Nefertiti asked.

"You saved *his* life, not mine," Lolli said. "And to answer your question, yes." She handed over the piece of paper.

Nefertiti steered with one hand and glanced down at the receipt. It was from a jewelry store called Schulman's Gold & Diamonds. She recognized Schulman as the surname of a Jewish gangster who was rumored to have snitched on Lolli's dad. The Porters had purchased a necklace from the store for twenty thousand dollars, which was later refunded.

"Okay, this establishes a connection between Alderman Porter and the Jew-snitch," said Nefertiti. "They did some business, but this was a refund, not a debt. The Porters didn't owe the Schulmans any money, so what reason would they have to whack the alderman, let alone pin it on your old man? I don't see it."

"Because you're ignoring the fine print," Lolli said.

Nefertiti looked closer at the receipt. There was a Porter name listed as the initial purchaser, but it wasn't *James*. Everything clicked into place. "Mu-tha-fucka . . ."

"That wasn't a refund—it was a payoff," said Lolli. What she hadn't shared with Nefertiti was that she had already known the connection between Mike and the Porter family, long before discovering the receipt. Lolli had come across the information quite by accident on the day she met with Alderman Porter about putting his support behind her father. While she'd been waiting for the alderman in his office, she'd some across a smaller print on his desk of the family portrait that hung on the living room wall. Seeing a much younger version of Mike with the Porter family had thrown Lolli for a loop. As far as she knew, Mike was a gangster who had pulled himself out of the mud, which was one of the things that had attracted her to him. She and Mike had been dealing with each other off and on for nearly two years. They were fuck buddies on the surface, but had also shared some very intimate moments. Lolli had trusted Mike with some of her darkest secrets and thought that he had done the same, but apparently he hadn't.

"I warned you about that nigga, Lollipop. He was always too pretty to be solid. We about to go back to that house and finish what we started." Nefertiti glanced at the passenger-side mirror to make sure she was clear before pulling a U-turn.

"For what?" Lolli said. "To get locked the fuck up? That gunshot probably attracted the police in that fancy-ass neighborhood, and we need to be thankful we got out of there before they showed."

"Like I give a crap about the police. I'm a Reaper . . . last of my line, and the blood of my mother. We born to die, Lolli, and the greatest reward someone like me can receive is losing our life in the service of those we're sworn to protect—or did you forget that?"

The Reapers were an elite death squad who had protected every head of the family since the days of Lolli's grandfather, Edward King. Uncle Colt had been the last commander of record for the Reapers, before he was murdered and the order eventually fell apart. Nefertiti had been Colt's apprentice and the last member ever admitted to the squad; she always felt like she needed to go the extra mile to prove herself.

"It ain't that I forgot," Lolli picked up, "it's that you're one of the few people who'd risk it all in the name of my family, which makes it impossible for me to let you sacrifice yourself." She laid her hand over Nefertiti's on the steering wheel. Their eyes met for only an instant, but long enough to convey the message. "Mike is a mess that I made and I'm going to clean it up. You can bet on that. Right now, he's only a small part of a bigger problem. I've been trying to drum up support for our effort, but it hasn't been going to well. A few are ready to stand with us, but most of the people who were loyal to my father have been pushed out, switched sides, or have chosen to sit on the sidelines and let it play out. Even men my brother has broken bread with and fed have turned their backs on us. How can we fight a war, let alone win one, with no army?"

Nefertiti shrugged. "Your Uncle Colt used to say, 'Sometimes you don't need an army, just a few solid muthafuckas who don't mind dying.'"

This made Lolli chuckle. "Colt had the Reapers. What do *I* have?"

"You have *me*! Lauren, I ain't gonna sit here and bullshit you like this is going to end well, because we both know it isn't. Fuck begging these so-called gangsters to do the right thing and stand tall. If I'm gonna die, I want it to be in your arms.

Me and you, baby . . . Let's take it to these muthafuckas and let God sort it out. All for the family."

The fire in Nefertiti's eyes burned so white-hot that it made Lolli's lady parts tingle. No man she had ever been with could do that to her with just a look. She made a note to herself that if they were fortunate enough to survive what they were planning, she would handle Nefertiti with more care in the future. Lolli took her bodyguard and sometime lover's hand and kissed the back of it softly. "All for the family."

PART III

My Brother's Keeper

CHAPTER 14

"Look at you boys, y'all as clean as the Board of Health!" an addict named Herm declared as he ambled up. He was tall and had always been thin, but drugs and hard living had him hovering somewhere between malnourished and skeletal. Back in the day, Herm had been a talented ball player, but he'd traded in hoop dreams for pipe dreams.

His comments were directed to a trio of neighborhood kids sitting on a stoop, the oldest being no more than nineteen. They were who you came to see when you needed narcotics, which is what had brought Herm out before sundown. His monkey couldn't sleep, so it wouldn't allow him to either.

"What's up with you, Herm?" one of the young men greeted with a friendly slap of his palm. This was Boone, a brown-skinned cat who wore his hair in fuzzy cornrows that always looked like they needed to be done over.

"Living like I do," capped Herm, "always out the way, and always in some pussy."

"You stay talking that talk!" Boone laughed. Herm may have been a junkie, but he was also a good dude with an infectious personality who could always make people smile.

Herm turned his attention to the kid sitting on the step below Boone. He had a splayed cigar laid across his palm and was breaking up buds of weed into it. "What up, Lou? How you living?"

"Better than you, nigga," Lou spat. He was light-skinned with a shaved head, and seemed to always be wearing a scowl.

"I swear, you gotta be the only nigga in the hood who just wakes up angry," Herm said. "Put a smile on your face, youngster."

"How about I put a smile on yours?" Lou removed a box cutter from his pocket.

"Chill, Lou," the third kid spoke up from the highest step. He had brown skin with chestnut eyes and thick lips that were never chapped. Three-sixty waves glistened atop his head in the afternoon sun. A modest gold chain hung from his neck with a depiction of St. Peter dangling from it. The sneakers on his feet were so white they looked like they had just come out of the box.

"See, that's why you've always been my man, Fresh. You always treat people with respect, no matter what their story is. Even when you started getting a little money out here, you didn't let it change you. Not like some people." Herm cut his eyes at Lou.

"I advise you to stop poking the bear and state your business. What you need?" Fresh asked. He liked Herm well enough, but he never lost sight of the fact that the man was an addict and, as such, liked to play dope-fiend games. With addicts, everything was always an angle.

"Can I talk with you for a minute, Fresh?" Herm asked.

Fresh shrugged. "Speak."

Herm hesitated. "In private . . . if it ain't too much trouble."

Fresh let out a sigh before standing. "Y'all hold it down. I'll be back in a second." He stepped between his two friends and off the stoop.

Boone waited until Fresh and Herm were out of earshot before turning to Lou. "Bro, why you always talking to Herm all crazy? He's an okay dude."

"Fuck that smoker," Lou said. "I'll be glad when he finally overdoses and drops dead."

Boone shook his head. "Herm might be out here on some bullshit, but it's kind of fucked up for you to wish death on your own father."

Fresh cut straight to the chase: "How many you need, Herm? And how much are you short this time?"

"Damn, man, why you automatically think I'm coming to you looking for a handout? For your information, I got money today." Herm reached into his pocket and pulled out some crumpled bills.

"Then why you fucking with me? Go cop from one of the little niggas like everybody else."

"I plan to," said Herm. "I'm gonna spend a little extra with y'all today because this will be my last ride. I'm getting clean."

"How many times have I heard this story?"

"I know, but I'm serious this time. Man, I been chasing the high for so long that I don't even remember what my life was like before it. The way they cutting drugs these days, it ain't even worth it no more. No offense," he chuckled. "But seriously, this is getting old and so am I. During whatever bit of time I got left, I'd like to remember what the world looks like through sober eyes. Take it back to a time before I became an embarrassment to my kids." He glanced in Lou's direction. "Just this month I've lost two of my running partners—one to an overdose and the other got his brains blown out trying to rob the wrong person. They say death comes in threes, and I'd rather not be the third. I'm done."

Fresh spared a look over his shoulder and found both Boone and Lou watching their exchange. "That's some heavy shit you just laid on me, Herm. But if you're serious, I can respect it. I appreciate you sharing this with me, though I'm not sure why you felt the need."

"Because I'm gonna need your help to do this. Well . . . really, your mom. I know she's had her . . . *struggles* in the past. Did a fine job of cleaning herself up for you kids. They say she still does work for some of them programs, huh?"

"Yeah, when she's not working her other two jobs, she volunteers at a rehab center out on Staten Island."

"That's why I'm coming to you," Herm said. "I was hoping maybe she could pull a string or two and get me a bed somewhere? I didn't want to come to you like this, but—"

"Say less," Fresh cut him off. "I'll speak to her tonight. I can't make any promises, but I'll at least have the conversation."

"That's all I can ask. Thank you, Fresh. On the real." Herm pulled him into an embrace. "I'm about to go get what I need so I can get to where I'm going. I'll spin back later to see what the word is." He started to walk off, but Fresh called after him.

"If this is really your last ride, the price of admission is on me. Tell my young boy to double down on whatever you planned to spend, but don't try and play me by going overboard. You got a hundred-dollar maker, and bet your ass I'm gonna check to make sure you didn't exceed it."

"Fresh, even an old fiend like me knows better than to try and cheat an angel of mercy. See you tonight." Herm saluted and headed over to the youngsters playing on the stoop. He said something softly to Boone, which led Boone to look over in Fresh's direction. Fresh nodded, letting him know that it was okay to bless Herm.

Fresh stood there watching Herm and Boone as they disappeared around the corner. He believed that Herm had been sincere in his promise to turn the corner and try to clean himself up, but didn't have a lot of faith in him following through. Especially after receiving one hundred dollars' worth of product for free. That was part of the reason Fresh had decided to give it to him on the arm. Herm wasn't your average addict. Whenever he came to cop, he had a story, something to trade, or three new fiends who were ready to spend their money with Fresh for the first time. What Herm brought to the table might've come in a trickle, but it was consistent. Some hustlers would look at the few dollars that Herm's hustles brought in as inconsequential, pennies instead of dollars. Not Fresh. Whether it jingled or folded, he needed it.

Fresh hadn't always been a mercenary. Until very recently, he had actually been a victim: a sheep hiding among the wolves. Then he had sprouted fangs of his own. From the influence Fresh had over the neighborhood he had once only lived in, but now controlled, you'd have assumed that he'd spent months or even years establishing himself there, but he hadn't. Flesh's backstory was one of microwaved success that had taken him from the outside looking in, to the inside calling shots. His current territory may have only consisted of one square city block, but considering that less than six months earlier he'd been selling loose dime bags for Chinese food and sneakers, his future was looking pretty good. There were a few who weren't happy with his rapid ascension, but that was because they didn't know what Fresh had sacrificed to get there.

"What he want, a blast on credit?" Lou asked once Fresh had returned to the stoop.

"No, a second chance."

Lou looked at Fresh as if he didn't understand his words, but before Fresh could elaborate, they heard gunshots.

CHAPTER 15

Fresh lay on the dirty concrete behind a car, heart thudding so hard in his chest that it was a miracle it hadn't jackknifed through the pavement. Lou was off the porch, 9mm in hand and eyes sweeping the block for signs of an attacker. Another shot went off. Fresh retrieved his own gun, a small .380 he kept stashed in his back pocket. He pulled himself into a crouching position and made his way over to Lou as Boone came running up. The three armed men watched the corner where the shots had come from and waited in anticipation. Ten seconds later, they spotted the source of the noises: not a gun, but backfires from the ugliest patchwork motorcycle any of them had ever seen, carrying two riders.

"You almost got blasted because of that piece of shit," Boone said, gun still in hand, as Pain dismounted the bike.

Pain looked from the 9mm back to Boone. "You wasn't gonna do shit."

"What? You don't think I'd let this thing bang?" Boone challenged.

"You might've tried," Pain said, "but it'd be hard to fire with the safety still on."

Boone checked the gun. "Fuck!"

"Fresh, you better get these little dudes some firearm training before one of them hurts themselves," Pain said, giving his friend a strong embrace. "You looking good, baby boy. I see you out here shining." He playfully flicked Fresh's gold chain.

"The game's been pretty good to me," Fresh said with a grin.

"Yeah, you've come a long way from back when we were out here selling shake to junkies."

Fresh laughed. "Yeah, we really thought we was out here doing something. No more kid games for me. It's grown-man business now." His eyes drifted to Shadow, who was leaning against the bike, watching.

Pain followed Fresh's line of vision. "Shadow, fuck you doing just standing over there? Come show our brother some love!"

Shadow hesitated before pushing himself off the bike. An awkward silence descended as Shadow and Fresh peered at one another. Neither of them spoke. For years, Shadow, Pain, and Fresh had been as thick as thieves. But Shadow and Fresh hadn't seen each other more than in passing since Ghost's funeral. It had only been a few months, yet it felt like years.

A lot had changed between the two childhood friends since then. Fresh was no longer the kid who liked to laugh and tell jokes, who looked to Shadow and Pain to keep the bullies off his ass. Physically, he was still the same person, but something inside him had shifted. Shadow could remember Ghost telling him that killing a man leaves a stain on your soul that can turn even the most gentle people into beasts. He never truly understood what his brother had been trying to tell him until he saw it happen to his best friend. A split-second decision had transformed a boy who Shadow had known since forever into a man who now felt like a stranger.

"Fresh," Shadow broke first, extending his hand.

Fresh glared at it for a few beats. "Fuck all that," he responded, and slapped Shadow's hand away. It looked like something might be about to go down between the two old friends, but Fresh pulled Shadow into a hug. "I don't care how long it's been since we've seen each other or what caused our rift, you're still my brother."

"And you're still mine," Shadow said.

"Ain't y'all the cutest?" Pain chimed in. "If you gonna kiss each other, let me get my phone out so you can do it for the 'gram."

"Fuck you, Pain!" Fresh took a friendly swing at him, but Pain danced out of his reach.

"Boy, don't play with me, you know I still got the fastest hands out here." Pain threw phantom punches. "Lil ass been on the block for a few months and now you think you're an OG."

"I wish I was getting OG money," Fresh said. "I got my little block to run, but I'm still out here doing soldier work."

"My cousin Monster ain't looking out for you?" Shadow asked. Since Ghost's murder, Monster had taken up his position as street general—the drugs Fresh and his boys were slinging came from his connect.

"Respectfully, Monster ain't looking out for nobody but Monster," Fresh said. "Honestly, though, I don't see him too much. I mostly deal with Judah."

"It's still weird to me to see that fool in a position of power," Pain said. "A few years ago, he was out snatching chains to feed himself."

"And so were you, yet here we are, right?" Fresh countered. "I ain't gonna lie, Judah a grimy dude, but he knows how to get to the money. He's been keeping me busy, which is why y'all ain't seen me around so much."

"Really? I thought it was because you shot a nigga with my mother's gun," Shadow half joked.

Fresh sighed. "You ain't never gonna let me live that down, are you?"

"I'm only fucking with you," Shadow told him, seeing that Fresh was in his feelings.

"Yeah, but a jab like that made more than once is sprinkled with a little truth."

"Not this shit again." Pain rolled his eyes. "I thought we agreed to leave the past in the past at the funeral."

"Some things ain't that easy to let go," Fresh said.

The incident in question had occurred on the same night as Maureen's birthday party, right before Chancellor's arrest. That morning, Fresh and a dude named Malice had gotten into it over Fresh's little sister. Shadow had stepped in and spoken on Fresh's behalf to get Malice off him, but Fresh was concerned that Malice might come back and press the issue at a later time. To put Fresh at ease, Shadow had loaned him his mother's personal gun. It was a small derringer that she kept hidden in the Benz that she had let Shadow borrow that morning. Shadow had only given the gun to his friend as a precaution. Fresh was the most nonconfrontational dude that Shadow knew and he never in a million years thought he'd need to pull the gun, let alone have the heart to use it. So it came as a shock to him when he got word that it had been his mother's gun that Fresh used to blow Malice's brains out.

"I tried calling you at least twenty times that night, but you never answered," Fresh said. "I don't know if I was looking for you to talk me into it or out of it. In hindsight, I could've let it be. I know you told me that you was going to have Ghost or one of the homies see about it to make sure it was officially over, but in the meantime, I would've had to look over my shoulder every time I left the house, hoping that crazy bastard didn't run down on me or try fucking with my sister again. Shadow, you've always had your dad or brother to look after you, so you don't know what it's like to live under that kind of pressure . . . knowing there's somebody out there who could end you anytime they felt like it, and there isn't shit you could do about it." He shook his head as his mind took him back to that day. "I just couldn't do it, Shadow. So instead of waiting for Malice to end me, I ended *him*."

Shadow measured Fresh's words. This wasn't the first time they'd had this conversation, but it was the first time Fresh had spoken so candidly about what drove him to cross that line. Even if Shadow wanted to blame Fresh, he couldn't. His friend was right: Shadow came from a family of predators, so he didn't have the slightest idea what it felt like to live as someone's prey.

"I'm sorry that I wasn't there for you when you needed me, Fresh. It's just that with the party and everything going on—"

"You don't owe me any explanation, Shadow. You had your own shit to deal with, and I understand that. What's done is done. My only regret about what I did that night is that I used your mom's pistol to do it. I could've jammed her and the rest of y'all up if that situation had played out different and Malice had gotten the drop on me instead of the other way around. For that, I am truly sorry. I wanted to apologize to her myself when I saw her at Ghost's funeral, but I felt like that wasn't the time or place."

"You good on that front," Shadow said. "With everything going on, it was a few days before she even noticed the gun was missing. I put in on Ghost. Ain't like she could've dug him up to see if I was lying or not. She's clueless about all this. The only reason I was able to put two and two together was because of

FALSE IDOLS

the caliber of gun Malice was killed with and me knowing y'all had issues. Your secret is safe with me."

Fresh nodded. "Thank you."

"If you really wanna thank me, make sure that gun never resurfaces. I don't need to tell you what kind of problems that could create, do I?"

"Not at all. That pistol is just as gone as Malice," Fresh said before changing topics to lighten the mood. "So, what brings y'all to the slums? I know you ain't pull up to check me, because I ain't seen either one of you ugly muthafuckas in ages."

"Actually, we did come to check you," Pain spoke up. "We need a solid."

"Shit, y'all know whatever is within my power, I'm gonna do for the team."

"Need some seed money for a start-up," Pain said. "Ain't asking for no cash, but maybe you can slide us a few grams on the arm and we'll see you later on for the balance?"

"Pain, last I heard, you hung up your dope-boy bag to become the prince of thieves. What happened? Queen Crow starving her little birds?"

"Fuck you, Frederick," Pain said, using his friend's government name. "I'm eating just fine. The ask ain't for me." He gestured toward Shadow.

"Shadow, you ain't no corner boy, you're royalty. Fuck you need with a package?"

Shadow could've snuffed Pain for putting him out there like that, but it was too late. So he spoke honestly: "Things are a little tight for me and Mom right now. I decided to get proactive."

"I don't mind hitting you with whatever," Fresh said, "but I gotta ask: why not just talk to Monster? You could bypass this hand-to-mouth shit and step into management."

"It's complicated," Shadow responded. "This is something I need to do on my own."

Fresh could read between the lines. There had been rumors about the King family's fall from grace, but until Shadow showed up today looking for a package, he hadn't realized how bad things had gotten for them. Fresh motioned Boone over and whispered something into the young man's ear. Boone gave him a quizzical look before going off to do as he was told.

A few minutes later, Boone came back carrying a brown paper bag, which he placed in Shadow's hand, before moving back to the stoop.

"That should bring you back about a grand to fifteen hundred. That's all depending on how you break it down. I'd hit you with more, but I don't wanna run the risk of throwing the count off any more than it already is."

"This is more than enough to get me started," Shadow said, shoving the package down into his pants. "I'll settle up with you as soon as I can."

"Don't worry about it. That's from me to you." Fresh touched his heart. "But if your cousin Monster catches you with that, you didn't get it from me."

CHAPTER 16

After the exchange with Fresh, Pain announced that he had to slide—the queen of the Crows had requested his presence. He offered to give Shadow a ride on his bike back to his building, but Shadow declined. Lou had just returned from the liquor store with a fifth of Henny, and Shadow was going to stay and help drink it. It had been too long since he and Fresh had hung out and he wasn't ready for the moment to end just yet.

Shadow kicked it on the stoop with Fresh, Boone, and Lou, drinking and firing up blunt after blunt. It felt like old times, and for a while Shadow was able to forget about his current set of problems. At that moment he was just a kid in high school again, hanging out with his friends and shooting the shit.

"Do you ever miss it?" he asked Fresh.

"What?"

"This." Shadow made a sweeping gesture. "Just out being young and dumb, without a care in the world."

"Honestly? I couldn't say. I've been the man of the house since way before Judah put me in position to get money. I had to help my mom and look after my baby sister. So aside from a few fleeting moments with my guys, my life has always been full of anxieties. I know shit is a little crazy with your family right now, but you should count your blessings."

"Why do you say that?" Shadow asked.

"Because of all of us, you were the only one who had a chance to be a kid."

Before their conversation could go any further, a white BMW X5 pulled up. From the way Boone and Lou jumped to their feet, you'd have thought it was carrying the president. Even Fresh stood up. The person who stepped out of the SUV might not have been the commander in chief of the United States, but he was a commander of the streets. Shadow had never met him in person, though he could guess from the way Fresh and the others tensed that this was the notorious Judah Friedman.

"'Sup wit' it, youngsters?" Judah greeted them.

"Chilling, big dawg," Lou replied. "Out here getting this money."

As Judah bypassed Lou and Boone and stepped to Fresh, his eyes landed on Shadow. "Y'all know how I feel about niggas I don't know being on the block when we out here doing business."

"This is my man Shadow," Fresh said. "He was just leaving."

"Shadow King? Ghost's little brother?"

"Yeah," said Shadow.

"It's an honor to meet you, shorty." Judah extended his hand. Shadow hesitated before taking it. "Your brother was a good dude. He put me in position to be great. I owe your family a lot. You ain't gotta leave. You good on any block I control."

"Shadow was just passing through," Fresh said. "You ready to go and handle that business?"

"We got a few minutes—why you in such a rush?" Judah

knew why Fresh was trying to usher Shadow off the block, and was just fucking with him. "So," he turned back to Shadow, "how's your family holding up these days? Any word on your dad?"

"We good."

"Glad to hear it. Listen, if y'all ever need anything, make sure you come see me. The big homie Monster made it clear that any member of the King family out here is to be taken care of without question."

"Thanks."

"No thanks necessary. Your family was royalty at one time, and the homies still getting money under the King flag. I'm actually surprised that you ain't jumped off the porch yet, considering that you're the last of your bloodline. You could be an important man out here, shorty. You a King."

"This ain't for Shadow," Fresh cut in. He didn't like the way Judah was looking at his friend. It was the same way he had looked at Fresh before recruiting him to kill Malice.

"Fuck is you, his mouthpiece?"

"I can speak for myself," said Shadow. "And I'm good." Fresh might've been one of Judah's soldiers now, but Shadow's protective instincts remained.

"Relax, Michael Corleone," Judah said. "I was just trying to see if you were ready to stop standing on the sidelines and get in the game."

"Are you hard of hearing?" a female voice joined the conversation. To everyone's surprise, Millie King came strolling out of the nearby African hair salon. She looked like a taller version of her mother, only thicker. Her hair was freshly braided and her weight was up. She had come a long way from the skeletal figure that had crashed Maureen's birthday dinner. Sobriety was definitely agreeing with her.

"Be cool, Millie," Judah responded. "I was just out here chopping it up with lil bro."

"Sounded like you were pissing in his ear to me," Millie shot back. "Shadow, Mom know you're on this side of town?"

"No. I'm grown, I ain't gotta report my whereabouts to her."

"Yeah, until something happens to you, and then she'll be the first one you call. Time for you to get up out of here, Sean." Millie knew what Judah and his gang were about and didn't want Shadow anywhere near them.

"Chill, Millie. I wasn't doing nothing, I'm just out here kicking it." She was blowing Shadow's high.

"Better listen to your big sister and run along, shorty," Judah said with a smirk. "Don't want her getting mad and telling your mother."

"Mind your fucking business," Millie snapped. "This is a family issue."

"Well, I thought I was family too, now that me and Monster are running the King family business on the streets."

Millie's eyes narrowed to slits. "Don't go there with me, Judah. You and that piece-of-shit cousin of mine better enjoy your fifteen minutes of fame while they last."

"And what's that supposed to mean? If I didn't know any better, I'd think you were threatening me. Don't let being sober make you forget who the fuck I am out here."

"I know just who you are, Judah, best believe that shit. But I think you might've forgotten who *I* am." Millie's hand slipped into her purse and came out holding a small gun. "This ain't strung-out Millie begging for a hit. This is Maureen's daughter Millicent, the same bitch who was out here making your big homies come off their jewelry."

Shadow and the younger guys had no clue what Millie was

talking about, but Judah knew all too well. Back when Millie first started getting high, she had run with a crew of robbers. They stuck up dealers and spots all over the city to feed their habits. Judah knew of three dudes who Millie and her people had done filthy. She was a female, but that didn't make her any less dangerous.

"You know what?" Judah said. "Out of respect for the King family, I'm gonna let you have that, Millie."

"Bullshit. You're gonna let me have it because you know that if you push me, I'm gonna push back." Millie tightened her grip on the pistol.

"Ain't no need for that," Fresh said. "Everybody chill."

Millie spun on Fresh. "You mind your business too. Like I told ya man, this is a family issue."

"So I ain't family no more?" Fresh had grown up around the Kings and they'd always treated him like one of their own.

"Honestly, I don't know what you are anymore," Millie said. "Especially considering the company you've been keeping lately. As many nights as you've eaten at my mother's table, I'd have thought better of you. Apparently, I gave you too much credit."

"Millie, whatever history you and Judah have, it's got nothing to do with Fresh," Shadow spoke up.

"Fresh might've never done no sucker shit to this family, at least that I know of, but standing next to a sucker tells me he condones that kind of behavior," Millie said with a snort. "Now, it's time for us to go, Sean."

Shadow didn't move right away. It was obvious that something was brewing between his sister and Judah. He couldn't say what it was, but the situation looked like it would escalate if they continued to hang around. On the other hand, he didn't want to lose face in front of the homies by letting his sister run him off at the first sign of tension. He was a King, and there was already enough dirt on his family's name without him adding to it by backing down from a potential fight. He realized he was locked in a game of chicken, but thankfully, Judah blinked first.

"I got better shit to do that stand around arguing with a fiend and her square-ass little brother. Let's make a move." Judah tapped Fresh on the arm and headed toward the X5 without looking back.

"I'm sorry about all that," Fresh said to the siblings.

"Ain't your fault." Shadow gave him dap.

"Ain't it?" Millie raised an eyebrow. "Go on off and follow your boss, but if I were you, I'd start trying to find gainful employment elsewhere."

"Meaning?" Fresh didn't know what the beef was between Judah and Millie. He was just unfortunately caught in the middle. Still, he didn't like how Millie was coming at him. He respected her because she was Shadow's half sister, but he didn't take impudence well these days.

"Hang around long enough and you might find out. Bring your ass on, Shadow, let's go!"

"What the fuck was that back there?" Shadow asked once he had caught up with Millie. She was making hurried steps down the street, hand out in an attempt to flag down a taxi.

"Me pulling you out of a fire before it starts." A yellow cab pulled to the curb and Millie jumped in the back, followed by her brother. She gave the driver Maureen's address and they were off.

"Oh, so now you concerned about your baby brother? Where was this concern for me, or even Mom for that matter, when you were running around not giving a fuck about nobody but yourself and embarrassing this family?" Shadow was upset and the words fell from his mouth before he'd had a chance to consider them.

Millie cut her eyes at him. There was a sharp response on her tongue, but she bit it back. She waited until she found the proper words before responding. "You right, Shadow. I spent more time chasing my vices than I did loving on my family, or allowing y'all to love on me. I was walking around in a cloud, but now that sobriety has lifted that fog from my brain, I see things with more clarity."

"And what does this new, sober Millie see that the rest of us weak-minded prisoners of our own vices can't?" Shadow was growing weary of Millie's drug-free condescension, which he had been subjected to for the last two months.

Millie peered at Shadow. He was posturing like a dude who had just capped something slick, but his eyes told a different story. One of uncertainty. It would've been the perfect opportunity to chastise the arrogant young prince and flog him with a handful of everything he thought he knew but didn't. Shadow had been spoiled by Maureen and Chance. He had never gone without and could benefit from a good humbling, but this wasn't the time. If Millie really wanted to help her little brother, she had to give him something that his parents, and all their wealth, had denied him . . . the truth.

CHAPTER 17

"*Truth*? What kind of name is that for a nail salon?" Malcolm read the name scribbled in silver letters across the black awning of the small building. He was a handsome dude, standing at about six two, with sandy blond hair and sharp blue eyes. People often remarked that he bore a striking resemblance to Lorenzo Lamas from the show *Renegade*.

"*Truth*? Looks more like a lie to me," kidded Marcus, who was Malcolm's twin brother.

Truth was advertised as a full-service spa, though it looked like an old department store that someone had done a half-assed job of renovating. If the inside resembled anything close to the outside, Marcus thought, they probably had more reported cases of staff infection than happy endings.

"In my time in the business, I've squeezed cash out of a lot worse places," said the third member of the trio. "Trust me on that." This was Marty, the current boyfriend of the twins' mother as well as their manager. He was a short, ruddy-faced man who always smelled like cigar smoke and sweat. You'd have never guessed that twenty years earlier he'd been a rising film star. A poor diet and even poorer financial decisions had tanked Marty's career, and he now picked up his coins wherever they fell.

The front door of the spa opened and out came a thin Asian man wearing a wrinkled business suit. He gave the three men a quick glance before lowering his head and moving past them, leaving the smell of sex and cheap body spray in his wake.

"Marty, this is insane," said Malcolm. "What kind of legit businessman does deals in a place like this?"

"The kind who's willing to pay your two broke asses with tax-free cash," Marty answered. "I had to pull a lot of strings to set this up. You two jokers have a lot of potential, but you're gonna need a little help to get to the next level. Now, if you don't like what you hear, you are free to go back to your lives making OnlyFans content in your mother's basement."

The twins exchanged a glance. Neither of them were comfortable being twenty-five and still leeching off their mother. They were desperate for the glorious lives they saw everyone else living when they scrolled through their social media.

"That's what I thought." Marty could see the desperation in their eyes. "When we get in there, you let me do all the talking. Your only jobs are to button your lips and look pretty."

As it turned out, the inside of the spa was easier on the eyes than the outside, though not by much. It was a wide space with a heavy black curtain separating the reception area from whatever was going on in the back. It was sparsely decorated with love seats on each side of the room. Sitting on a coffee table was a dime-store vase filled with plastic flowers and some outdated magazines. The floors were lined with imitation marble, and the walls were painted a drab yellow. It must've been a fresh job because there was still a chemical taint in the air.

At the mouth of the curtain there was an OfficeMax-quality desk. Behind it sat a curvaceous Mexican woman wearing a dress that was more suited for a night on the town than a day at the office. She was over fifty, quite pretty, and wore her hair in a blond beehive. She was chatting away on her phone with a big grin on her face. When she saw the trio walk in, she moved the phone to her shoulder and turned her attention to the guests. "Can I help you?"

"Marty Shultz. Mr. Knight should be expecting me." He shot the cuffs of his suit, feeling like a heavyweight.

After a pause and a once-over, the receptionist got up from the desk and disappeared behind the curtain. She was only gone for a minute or two, but it felt to the twins like an hour. When she reemerged, she wasn't alone. Trailing her was a rail-thin man with skin the color of charred wood, dressed in a white shit. His processed hair was combed back, drawing attention to his high forehead. "He's ready for you," the man said, pulling the curtain aside with a bony hand.

Marty and Marcus moved past, followed by Malcolm, who spared a glance at the white-clad man and thought he saw a smile touch the corners of the guy's mouth.

The twins had been expecting to be led into some fiery pit of hell, but instead their journey ended in a parlor. It was slightly larger than the room they had just left, with hardwood floors instead of the imitation marble of the reception area. There were several armchairs set along the wall, and occupying the closest was one of the biggest men either twin had ever seen. The guy's face was buried in a newspaper, but as they entered, he looked up. It was only a brief stare of acknowledgment, yet his dead eyes sent chills down the backs of all three visitors.

The man in white ushered them deeper into the parlor.

There were nail stations set up on each side of the room, and three chairs reserved for pedicures at the back, under a large window looking out on the apartment buildings behind the spa. Sitting in one of these chairs was a man of slender build. He was dressed in a peach linen suit with the pant legs rolled up to his knees. One foot was submerged in a bucket of water, with the other propped on the rim of the bucket while a young woman scrubbed his heel vigorously with a brush. Another woman was applying a coat of clear nail polish to the man's fingers, while a third stood behind him smoothing gel into his finger-waved hair.

The two nail girls were cute, but the one working on his hair, not so much. There was something about her facial features that was a bit too hard. They didn't seem to match the long black wig spilling down her back. She and the man in the chair were engaged in a conversation, which was brought to a halt when the three men approached. There was an uncomfortable pause while the man regarded his guests.

The ghoulish man who had escorted them in cleared his throat and spoke: "You are now in the presence of our esteemed benefactor, Christian Knight, el Príncipe de la Noche!"

"Luther," said Christian with a chuckle, "why must you always announce me like you're Ed McMahon and I'm Johnny Carson?"

"By using your proper title," Luther replied, "I'm merely showing respect to your station, same as I always have." When Christian had first found Luther, he'd been a resident of a dope house that had been condemned by the Monarchy. This was when Christian had still been Ghost's understudy. Christian and his gang had been tasked to carry out the order, and they did so with efficiency. Luther had been the only survivor of the massacre, thanks to the mercies of Christian. Instead of killing the addict, Christian had cleaned him up and given him a job. To that day, only Christian knew why he had spared the life of the old dope fiend. Whatever his reasons, Luther was forever thankful and demonstrated this through his fierce loyalty to Christian and his cause.

"I know, my friend," Christian flashed his perfect smile, "but that was back when nobody knew my name. These days, it's on everyone's lips." He now turned his attention back to the visitors. "Nice to see you again, Marty. Especially fully clothed and without someone trying to take your head off with a baseball bat."

Marty winced. The last time he'd seen Christian face-to-face, he'd been in a bad way. Marty had made the mistake of trying to purchase some cocaine from two of Christian's young associates. The problem was, he had attempted to make the buy with counterfeit bills. The young boys had stripped Marty out of his clothes and given him an ass-whipping he wouldn't soon forget. The only reason they hadn't kill him was because Ghost had shown up somewhat randomly and didn't want to catch a body in one of the spots where he generated his money.

"I was a different person back then," Marty said. "I got my shit together now."

"I should hope so, because Ghost ain't here no more to get in the way of your karma," Christian said, then addressed the women working on his feet: "Ladies, take five while I handle this right quick." One headed toward the reception area of the parlor, while the other slipped out a back door for a cigarette break. The woman working on his hair remained. "So, these are the young studs you can't seem to shut up about? What do you guys call yourselves again—the Parker Brothers?"

"Actually, it's the Park-*Her* Brothers," Marcus said, rotating his hips.

Christian rolled the name over in his head. "I like that."

"Christian, these boys are the truth," said Marty. "Their last two-on-one OnlyFans video has gone viral and racked up almost two million views in just two or three weeks. Even Porn-Rub has shown interest in acquiring some of their content."

"PornRub?" Christian said. "If one of the biggest sites in the game is interested in your boys, why bring them to me?"

"Because you can do with them what a commercial site can't. Having a large machine behind my boys ain't a bad thing, but with a company that big, they'll probably only see pennies. Everyone knows that the Prince of the Night has access to doors that the corporate adult entertainment industry can't enter."

"You mean are *afraid* to enter," Christian said. "I'll admit, you boys are pretty enough that I'm sure that I could turn a profit—but what makes you special? Why should I put my money behind you?" Marty started to reply, but Christian waved him silent. "Marty, you could sell water to a whale. Let *them* sell me."

The twins looked at each other, not sure what to say. Marty was the mouthpiece, so they had no idea how to sell their own brand.

When a look of boredom crossed Christian's face, Malcolm finally took the initiative. He unzipped his pants and pulled out his cock.

"Sweet lord!" the woman working on Christian's hair gasped. They would later find out that the stylist's name was Jessie; she was a trans woman who had been by Christian's side since she was a teen.

"That is quite a bit of meat," Christian said. The penis was at least ten inches and nearly as thick around as a ping-pong ball.

"*Bit* of meat? Baby, that's an oven stuffer!" The hair stylist fanned herself.

"Take it easy, Jessie girl," Christian said. "I don't think these boys swing that way. Though if they did, the possibilities could be endless."

"Nah, we ain't into the homo shit," Marcus said.

Jessie's voice dropped three whole octaves: "White boy, I can guarantee I'm more woman than your mama, and surely more gangsta than your stepdaddy. Watch your fucking mouth before I force something into it."

"Tuck them fangs, Jess," Christian soothed. "Boy ain't mean no harm. Just letting you know he don't bend that way." He turned to Marty and the twins. "Now, why don't we sit and have a drink while I tell you boys how I'm going to make you stars."

Christian's sale's pitch was interrupted when the back door to the spa opened. It was the nail tech who had stepped outside to take her smoke break. Only now she wasn't alone. Three men stormed into the place. Christian didn't recognize the first two, but the third was Cheese, Judah's right-hand man. Even if Christian hadn't seen the weapons in their hands, he'd have known what this was about.

"How many times do I have to tell you broads to make sure that back door stays locked when you go out?" Christian scolded, ignoring the armed men. "That's how the rats get in. You know how much those exterminators charge whenever I have to call them out."

"A rodent problem should be the least of your concerns right now," Cheese said, hefting his gun around as if it wasn't already visible. "Monster gave you a deadline and your time is officially up."

"Right, the whole get-down-or-lie-down thing," Christian

said. "I know that your boss is a bit on the slow side, which is why I made sure to use small words when I told him I won't bend over and be fucked by a false king."

"You say that like you got a choice," said John, one of the other two gunmen. Cheese had warned his subordinates to stay back and follow his lead, but John was trying to make a name for himself.

Christian looked at John like he was a puppy nipping at the hem of his pants. "Sweet baby, you ain't never heard the expression about keeping your mouth closed when grown people are talking? Cheese, why don't you send these little green niggas outside and maybe me and you can have a civil conversation?"

"I think the time for talking is over." Cheese pointed his gun at Christian. "The way I see it, you got two options: fall in line with the rest of what's left of the King soldiers, or come up missing. Don't matter to me. I never liked your homo ass anyhow."

"Well, that's just too bad, Cheese, because I always had a soft spot in my heart for your ugly ass. Because of that, I'm going to ignore your disrespect and be merciful by making your deaths as painless as possible." Christian held up two fingers.

Cheese heard the sound of glass shattering a moment before the head of the third gunman exploded. More glass cracked when a second bullet whistled right into John's neck. John staggered left to right like he was drunk, clutching at his throat with both hands. The gun he'd been holding was now abandoned on the ground. John had always boasted to Cheese and Judah that he wanted to die in the streets, but he was instead taking his last breaths in the back of a nail salon.

"Thank you, Boogie," Christian called out to the other side of the broken window. Boogie was another one of Christian's reclamation projects, though he came with an invaluable skill set: he was an ex–army sniper who could shoot the wings off a fly from twenty yards out. Christian had stationed him in the window of one of the apartments behind the spa for the past several hours. The Prince of the Night was a firm believer in always carrying an insurance policy.

When Christian had gotten word of the brazen move Monster had made by killing his people in the trap house, he immediately knew what the play was. He was trying to draw Monster out by making it personal. This was a tactic they had both learned while studying under Ghost. Both had proven to be excellent students in the art of war, though Monster's greatest weakness had always been something he lacked, which Christian had in abundance: patience. Christian knew that a well-baited trap would be something that his former comrade wouldn't be able to resist. And Monster did not disappoint.

When John fell dead at Cheese's feet, the gunman snapped out of his shock. His first instinct was to raise his weapon back up and fire at Christian. There was no question in his mind that he was going to die that afternoon, but at least he'd take one of his enemies with him. As his hand slowly ascended, Christian simply watched him with an amused expression on his face. They could bury the fairy with that dumb-ass smirk on his face, as far as Cheese was concerned. So long as Cheese was written into the history books as the one who had murdered the Prince of the Night, a man who was said to be unkillable. His gun was now level with Christian's face. Cheese's finger was caressing the trigger when his world was dismantled.

Cheese didn't actually feel any pain until a second or two after his wrist was broken. A massive hand covered his forearm from wrist to damn near elbow. He opened his mouth to scream, but the wind was knocked out of him when he was slung halfway across the room. Cheese crashed into a wall, landed on his ass, and began drifting in and out of consciousness; he could see flashes of an enromous shadow stalking toward him. As Cheese's vision cleared and he took in the man's hideous features, he wished he had stayed unconscious. When he was snatched up and slammed against the wall, he realized the man had to be somewhere around six six or six seven. The wide face had a crooked nose and a scar shaped like a lightning bolt over one of his dark eyes. A huge hand clamped around Cheese's neck and cut off his wind, then came the sounds of joints popping. It felt like his head was about to be separated from the rest of him. He prayed that he would pass out before that happened.

"That's enough, Frank," Christian finally spoke up.

Frank, also known as Frankenstein because of his resemblance to the creature, looked over one of his wide shoulders at his boss. He still held Cheese's throat in his hand, but had stopped applying pressure. "Hardly," he said in a voice that sounded like two chain saws dueling. "How many of these misguided sheep we gonna let come onto our land without slaughtering and cooking at least one?" He gave Cheese a shake, sending pain running down his neck and through his limbs.

"Ain't enough meat on the bones of that one to feed your big-ass appetite, Frank. Throw him back."

Frank mumbled something under his breath before letting Cheese fall to the ground, gasping for air.

Christian removed his foot from the bucket and shook the water off before rising from the chair. He plodded barefoot across the hardwood floor, leaving a trail of wet footprints behind him. He stopped short of where Cheese lay in a heap, peering up with terror in his eyes. Christian shook his head. "The least Monster could've done was show me the respect of sending someone who had an actual shot at harming a hair on this pretty head of mine." He patted his waves. "You rank amateurs are a testament to just how far down into the shitter Chapman has been allowed to drag the Monarchy."

"You gonna chastise this muthafucka or are we gonna kill him?" Frank asked.

Christian ignored the comment and addressed Cheese: "Recently, someone very dear to my heart came to me for a favor and I turned them away. I thought that if I watched the sunset from the shade while everyone else stood directly in the light, I wouldn't get burned. I was wrong. You coming here and pissing on my shoes is proof of that." He gave Frank a nod.

Frank lifted Cheese up and forced him to his knees. He held Cheese's wrists behind his back in one of his massive hands and ripped open the front of his shirt with the other. There was a tattoo of his son's mother's name inked across his chest.

Without taking his eyes off Cheese, Christian held out his palm. Jessie immediately handed over a pair of barber's shears. "I've heard the false king's offer. Now, here is my counter."

CHAPTER 18

The sun had long set by the time Lolli made it back to her apartment building. She had been pounding the pavement with Nefertiti all day, turning over every rock and shaking every tree, and still felt no closer to solving her family's troubles. In fact, things had taken a turn for the worse.

Nefertiti had dropped Lolli off so that she could freshen up and regroup while the last of the Reapers returned to the matter at hand. The woman had a motor that just wouldn't quit. But Lolli understood Nefertiti's sense of urgency. They were running out of time and options. It had been months since two of the men she loved most had been taken from her, and her worm of an uncle had been strutting around wearing her daddy's crown. The longer Chapman was allowed to stay in power, the harder it would be to remove him. They needed to come up with a way to depose him from the Monarchy before his hold became absolute. Yet every time Lolli felt like they were getting close, life threw another curveball. The latest one had come in the form of a heartbreak.

Every time she thought back on what she had discovered, it hurt a little more. How could he? She wasn't naïve enough to think that she and Mike were more than but fuck buddies, so he didn't owe her any loyalties in that way, but there had always been a mutual respect between them. At least that's what Lolli had assumed. What she had found at that big house in Ridgefield Park told her differently. All this time, Mike had been fucking her in more ways than one.

Lolli now knew that Mike was a player in the game—but what was his position? The receipt provided a connection between Mike and Paul Schulman, the man who had framed her father, though to what end? If Schulman was able to pin the death of the alderman on Lolli's dad, this meant that he had intimate knowledge of what really happened. It was possible that it had been Schulman himself who'd killed the alderman after Lolli left, but something about that theory didn't sit right. Lolli didn't know Schulman personally, but from what she'd heard, he was someone who'd rather have other people do his dirty work than soil his own hands. Either way, he was the missing link to proving her father's innocence.

The receipt also raised an even bigger question: if Schulman had been responsible for the murder of Alderman Porter, why was Mike in bed with him? She knew from past conversations that Mike didn't have the best relationship with his father, but doing business with the man who'd had him killed was a whole different level of family dysfunction. None of it made sense, which meant there was something that Lolli was overlooking. There were only two people who could fill in the blanks, and Lolli planned to kill them both at her earliest convenience.

When she stepped off the elevator onto the floor of her apartment, she heard her stomach growl. It was a reminder that she hadn't eaten all day. That was a bad habit Lolli had picked up since her life had been turned upside down: going all day with only liquor and thoughts of revenge to fuel her. She considered stopping by her mom's to check on her and see if she had cooked something up, but decided against it. She knew if she went there she would be good for a meal, but it also meant she'd get an earful of Maureen's bullshit. She loved her mother dearly, but the woman had a one-track mind, and lately she'd become obsessed with taking back what belonged to them by any means necessary.

Maureen had probably taken Chapman's fall from the throne the hardest. With good reason. The Monarchy had been *her* vision, not Chance's. She been the one to plant the seeds for her husband to water. Lolli could only imagine what it must've felt like for her mother to have something she'd helped to grow from infancy so abruptly snatched away from her. Lolli worried about her mother—this woman who had once been so full of life had been reduced to brooding, drinking, and plotting to pass her days. Much like her daughter.

By the time Lolli reached her apartment door, she was on autopilot. She swiped her key fob across the lock and let herself in, then stopped in the foyer to relieve herself of the combat boots she'd been wearing all day. Her feet offered up silent thanks for the tender mercy. When she went to pull off her hoodie, pain shot through her side. She flicked on the light and lifted the hoodie to examine herself in the full-length mirror mounted near her front door. She turned this way and that, checking out the bruises from her fight with Mike. It would be awhile before she was able to wear a top that showed off any skin.

Lolli was wrapping up her inspection when something caught her eye in the mirror. From where she was standing, she could see the guest bathroom door a few feet behind her. The door was closed but a strip of light showed beneath it, and she was certain she hadn't left any lights on when she split that morning. As she slipped her chrome P89 out of the holster hooked to the back of her jeans and tiptoed toward the bathroom, she heard the toilet flush, followed by the sound of the faucet running. What kind of burglar bothered to wash their hands while robbing someone's home? She took a step back before raising her gun so that the blood wouldn't get on her when she blew the intruder's head off.

The door opened just as Lolli squeezed the trigger. At the very last moment, she shifted her aim and the bullet went high, striking the bathroom wall just above the head of the man stepping out.

"What the fuck, Lolli!" Trembling, Shadow looked from his sister to the smoking hole in the wall. "You could've killed me!"

"And it would've served you right! How the hell did you get into my apartment?"

"With the spare key you gave Mom for emergencies." Shadow fished around in his pocket and pulled out a key fob.

"Yes, for *emergencies*. Not for your simple ass to invade my space." Lolli snatched the fob. "And I hope you ain't got one of your hood rats up in my spot."

"Nah, just me." Shadow brushed past Lolli and headed into her kitchen.

"Damn, boy, you smell like Ned the freaking Wino. Fuck you been drinking?"

"Hope you don't mind, but I helped myself to your liquor cabinet." Shadow pointed to a bottle of Glenfiddich 18 on the counter.

Lolli scooped up the expensive scotch. She'd only cracked it to take a few shots on her last birthday, but now there was a healthy dent in the bottle. "Boy, of all the regular liquor I got in here, you had to fuck with my high-end shit? You're gonna buy me another one. You always touching my shit!"

"I got you, Lolli. Damn! Why is it that all the women in this family do is beef?"

"Because the men in this family don't listen."

Shadow muttered something to himself before picking up the glass he'd been sipping from and taking another swig.

Lolli was about to lay into him about his flippant attitude and violating her privacy, but paused. Something about her brother seemed off. "You okay, Shadow?"

He flopped into one of the chairs at her breakfast nook and finished off his glass before finally saying, "Honestly? I don't even know."

Lolli set the P89 on the counter, grabbed another glass from the rack, poured some whiskey into it, then refreshed Shadow's drink. "Talk to me, little brother. What's on your heart?"

Shadow ran his finger around the glass before taking a small sip. When he looked up, his eyes were moist. He wasn't crying, but not far from it either. "Did you know?"

Lolli didn't need him to elaborate—the pain painted across his face said it all. "I'd heard what the streets were saying, but I wasn't totally sold. At least not in the beginning."

"And now?"

Lolli thought back to the receipt and the unexplained connections. "Yeah, it was an inside job. Who told you—Mom?"

"She dropped a few hints, but it was Millie who gave it to me raw." Shadow recalled the cold dose of reality Millie had thrown in his face during their cab ride. He had heard the whispers, same as everyone else, but couldn't bring himself to believe them until Millie filled in the blanks as to what had really happened to Ghost. She'd gotten the information from one of her old crackhead buddies who'd been on the scene when the murder went down. By the time Millie was done relating the details, Shadow had been physically ill. So ill that he had thrown up on the steps of their building. That was when he decided to jump on the train and head to Lolli's crib. There was no way he could have faced Maureen right then, not after what he'd just learned. "I'm gonna kill him, you know. Monster first, but I'm gonna whack all four of them, if I'm being honest. Every fingerprint on Ghost's death is getting scrubbed off. I'm talking serial-killer territory with this one."

"Calm down, Shadow. You ain't about to kill nothing, so stop that kind of talk. You need to relax and let people more qualified to handle this type of shit see about it."

"More qualified people like *who*? Them same sucker niggas playing the background in our time of need like Daddy and Ghost ain't the ones who elevated them from three-piece chicken boxes to steak? Lolli, these niggas put our daddy in prison and killed our brother. Ain't nobody more qualified to bathe in their blood than *me*!"

"Shadow, I doubt anybody other than Mom has taken this harder than me, so I feel your pain. I promise you I do, but—"

"Hold on, big Sis. Unless it was *you* who just spent the last few hours passing blunts and sharing liquor with the men responsible for your big brother's death, you couldn't possibly feel my pain. You know what kind of sucker I feel like right now?" He thought back to Fresh smiling in his face on that stoop, and the whole time he'd been making money with the man who murdered Ghost.

"Yeah, I think I know a little bit of something about feeling like a sucker." An image of Mike popped up in her brain. "Look, Shadow, regardless of how either of us feel about it, I doubt there's anything we can do tonight. But tomorrow is a different animal."

When Lolli's cell phone vibrated in her pocket, she pulled it out to find a text message from someone she hadn't expected to hear from. It was short and to the point. Lolli placed her phone on the table and turned her attention back to her brother. "Crash here tonight. We'll order some DoorDash and plan this like a family. I got some shit in motion that's gonna turn the tide of this little skirmish, but I need you to trust me and stay out of the way. Can you do that?"

"I guess." Shadow shrugged.

Lolli opened the DoorDash app on her phone, then slid it over to Shadow. "I'm about to jump in the shower right quick, but in the meantime, you can figure out what we're gonna eat."

"If it's on you, I'm about to see if any seafood spots are delivering over here. I could go for steak and lobster," Shadow said with a small twinkle in his eye. He was still mad as hell, but being able to vent to Lolli had already made him feel a little better.

"You got a thirty-five-dollar limit, lil nigga, so don't get too crazy." Lolli got up from the breakfast nook and headed toward the bedroom. Then she stopped and turned back to her little brother. "Thank you for trusting me."

"If not you, then who?" Shadow smiled at his sister.

Lolli stayed in the shower far longer than she had planned to. She bowed her head under the hot spray and let it wash away her failures from the day. She was upset with Millie for spilling the beans to Shadow about what had really happened to their brother. Ghost and Monster had been Shadow's heroes, so she could only imagine how hard he was taking it that Monster had been the one to set up their brother. Monster had never been one of her favorite people when they were growing up. There was something in the way he had stared at her when he thought she wasn't looking that had creeped her out. Yet she had never thought of him as disloyal. He and Ghost were more like brothers than cousins. Ghost had been taking care of Monster since he was little, and Monster paid him back by snaking him. When Lolli caught up with her cousin, she planned to take her time in killing him. A quick death would be too merciful.

Millie had been wrong for telling Shadow without discussing it with her or Maureen first, but how long had they thought they'd be able to keep the truth from him? Shadow wasn't slow and the streets talked, so it would have only been a matter of time before he put two and two together on his own, but still . . . On the flip side of that, Shadow had as much right to know what really happened as anyone. After all, he was the last of them—Chancellor King's only remaining male heir—and should have been the one sitting on the throne, not Uncle Chapman. Even if her little brother was unprepared to take up the mantle of leadership, the crown was still his by right of succession. Shadow discovering the truth had thrust him right into the thick of things. He was a piece on the board now, and it was Lolli's responsibility to teach him how to move.

After her shower, Lolli sat on the edge of her bed and began drying herself off while reviewing her mental checklist of things she needed to do. She would call Maureen and tell her what her big-mouthed daughter had done. Their mother would probably be happy that Shadow finally knew. She had always been trying to push him toward the family business, despite their father's protests. Lolli was actually surprised that she hadn't already told him, forcing her little brother's hand. Maureen was manipulative like that. Sometimes Lolli felt like her mother loved the power that came with being queen more than she loved her husband.

"Shadow, how long did they say before the food gets here?" Lolli called out while slipping on a pair of sweatpants.

There was no response.

"Shadow?" she called again.

Still no response.

Lolli put on a tank top and moved back to the kitchen. All the liquor Shadow drank had probably kicked in and she expected to find him passed out on the couch—but there was no sign of him. Maybe he had gone downstairs to grab the food from the delivery guy?

She found her phone on the counter with her Messenger app open. There was an opened text from an unknown number that had come in ten minutes earlier: *Lauren, here you will find a copy of "Where the Wild Things Are."* It was accompanied by a location and time, and ended with a crown emoji.

Lolli had an idea who had sent the text. There were few people who called her Lauren outside of business meetings, and fewer still who knew that *Where the Wild Things Are* had been one of her favorite books since she was a kid. She had lost her copy when her apartment flooded a few years back, but was gifted another one two birthdays ago. It would take more than a book to get him back into her good graces after what she'd learned. She was about to set the phone down when something occurred to her: she wasn't being led to a book, she was being led to a monster.

She needed to get ahold of Nefertiti so they could gather the troops and ride out. Lolli started to dial her number, but stopped. The message had already been read by the time she saw it, which meant Shadow had seen it too. A sickening feeling came over her and she turned back to the counter where she had left her P89. The gun was gone too.

CHAPTER 19

The vehicle was whipping its way through traffic en route to the Bronx, with Judah behind the wheel and Fresh riding shotgun. Judah had a blunt dangling from one side of his mouth, humming along to an old Nas cut playing on the radio. He was in an unusually upbeat mood, though the same couldn't be said for Fresh. He had been morose ever since the situation earlier with Shadow.

"You hear this shit, shorty?" Judah said, turning the song up. "That's *real* hip-hop. Fucking bars! It ain't nothing like that mumble-mouth shit y'all be riding around with. That shit sounds like if you listen to it long enough, you'll get brain damage." He turned to Fresh, who was staring out the window lost in his own thoughts. "You good over there?"

Fresh glanced at him. "Yeah, I'm straight."

"Don't seem so. We're on our way to a meeting that could potentially change your fucking life, and you sitting over there pouting like a girl who got stood up on prom night. What's going on?"

This time Fresh didn't just glance, he stared right at Judah. "What was that shit back there? Why you get at my people like that?"

Judah sucked his teeth. "Man, you tripping off me getting at your homeboy's sister on some bullshit? That wasn't about nothing. You know how these fiends are when they get sober. They act like they ain't just have their lips wrapped around a pipe or a needle in their arm, like they better than everybody else. I was just reminding Millie of where she came from."

"Sounded like it was deeper than you checking a former fiend. That shit felt personal."

"Meaning what? If you got something on your heart, get it off." Judah didn't like the direction the conversation was going.

Fresh thought about how to respond and decided to shoot straight: "Y'all had something to do with what happened to Ghost?" He had heard chatter on the streets about Judah's possible involvement, but hadn't paid it any attention until the exchange with Millie. Things were no longer adding up right.

"You really gonna ask me some shit like that?" Judah said.

Fresh remained silent.

"Ghost was the big homie," Judah went on. "He put a lot of niggas in position to get money. He was loved out here."

"You still ain't answered my question: did you kill my best friend's brother?"

Fresh was a sharp kid and well tapped into the streets, so Judah figured this was a conversation they'd eventually need to have, but not this soon. He had that bitch Millie to thank for it. "If you wasn't my lil man, I'd shoot you in the face for asking such a disrespectful question. The only reason I'm even entertaining you enough to speak on this is because I don't want to see you make the same mistake. Ghost was a superstar out here, but he got so caught up in his own hype that he thought the laws of the jungle no longer applied to him. The natives showed him different. I know it sounds harsh, but that's the game. We play it and reap the benefits, but in the end, there are no real winners. Death or prison is in all of our futures, including *yours*. Ghost took his eye off the ball and struck out. Let what happened to him be a lesson to all you young niggas on the come-up."

"Trust me, my head is always on swivel," Fresh said. He hadn't missed the fact that Judah still hadn't given him a direct answer.

"That's good, because the minute you get caught slipping, you're gonna be another casualty. Where's all this coming from anyhow? Before today, you was out here smiling and stuffing your pockets like the rest of us. Now you all in your feelings and asking questions with answers that don't concern you. What, you having seconds thoughts about all this? If so, I can drop you back off where I found you: living off your mama and hiding behind the Kings' skirts for protection. Victims don't last long out here."

"I ain't no victim."

"I guess you ain't," said Judah. "At least not since I helped get Malice off your ass. Or has your reunion with your little friend given you amnesia?"

Fresh remembered all too well how he had ended up in bed with Judah. Fresh had become familiar with Judah back when Judah and Fresh's older brother Kevin used to rob gas stations together, so he didn't think too much of it when Judah approached him offering a solution to the problem he was having. According to Judah, he had heard through the grapevine that Fresh had been having some issues with Malice. Apparently, Judah wasn't a fan of Malice either, and him out there trying to bully Kevin's little brother was reason enough for Judah to do something about it. Fresh was suspicious of Judah's offer, but he was more worried about what Malice might do to him, so he'd accepted.

The plan had been for Fresh to hide in Malice's lobby while Judah and Cheese ran him down. Once they had him trapped, they were just going to give him a good beating. Fresh realized that he'd been lied to as soon as he heard the shooting. He watched from his spot in the lobby as Judah chased Malice to the building, and as dumb luck would have it, one of the other tenants was coming out at the same time, which allowed Malice to escape into the safety of his building's lobby. What happened next unfolded like an out-of-body experience. Fresh saw himself step from the shadows just as Malice turned to go up the stairs. Fresh raised the gun that Shadow had loaned him, his hand trembling. He hadn't intended to shoot Malice, only scare him, but when he saw the menacing glint in the other man's eyes, he knew it would never be over until one of them was dead. So he pulled the trigger. That was the first time Fresh had shot a man, though it wouldn't be the last.

"No, I didn't forget what you done for me, Judah. And I'm grateful, but let's not act like you didn't want Malice dead as much as I did." Several weeks after the killing, Fresh learned that Judah had landed on Ghost's shit list. For what? He still wasn't sure, but what he did know was that Ghost had charged Judah with the task that Fresh had completed.

"Tomato, tomahto, nigga. What's important is: those who need to be gone are gone, and we out here getting this money! Now, pull your panties up and stop crying. We almost there."

in the King vehicle, he was informed that the location had been moved, and Chapman neglected to share any details. Now Dickey found himself alone and unprotected, riding in the back of a luxury truck wedged between a snake and a gorilla, about to be marched into the unknown. He was familiar with both names listed on the sign. Chapman was the king of Five Points, but Shai Clark's reach was the king of kings. Meeting on Clark's property made no sense. This was Monarchy business, or so Dickey had been led to believe. His father's words about him being too ambitious came back to him, and he couldn't help but wonder if he had overplayed his stroke.

"Relax, Dickey," said Chapman. "If you're worried that we're about to walk you into something sinister that'll find that tight little Italian ass of yours in a sling, you needn't be. It was actually my nephew's idea to switch things up. I just picked the new location. A friend of ours in the King organization is graciously allowing us the use of this site to handle our business."

Dickey looked to Monster for further explanation.

"Just a precaution," Monster said. "At the meeting earlier, my uncle might've gotten the impression that not everyone's on the same page. So the last-minute switch was meant to throw any potential dogs off our scent. Not even soldiers loyal to the Monarchy are bold or stupid enough to spill blood somewhere Shai Clark has laid claim to, even an unfinished patch of dirt. This will keep everybody honest."

"Always two steps ahead, huh, Monster?" The lumbering ox was obviously sharper than Dickey had given him credit for.

Monster laughed. "Nah, nigga. *Three*."

Judah parked his whip two blocks away, and they walked from there to the location where the meeting was to be held. He looked at the time on his phone and cursed—they were run-

CHAPTER 20

"This wasn't the agreed-upon meeting spot," Dickey said from the backseat of the King SUV. The vehicle had just pulled to a stop in front of a construction site in Sunset Park, Brooklyn. They seemed to be building some type of housing development on a plot of land that stretched two city blocks in either direction. The sign on the front read, *Clark Lansky Realty.*

"Plans are subject to change," Chapman said. "You should know that better than anybody, Dickey."

The original plan had been for all parties involved to meet at a steakhouse in Midtown. Dickey knew the place well enough and his father had connections in the neighborhood, so he felt comfortable rolling in with his muscle, Big Dave. At the last minute, Chapman had personally reached out to inform him that he would be riding in the King vehicle. Dickey assured him that he could make his own way; he still needed to pick up Big Dave, and didn't trust riding with the Kings alone. But the new king of Five Points had insisted.

Dickey had immediately called Big Dave and told him to head to the steakhouse. To his surprise, however, when he got ning a few minutes behind. But it wasn't his fault. He had been early for the meeting and looking for parking near the steakhouse when he noticed the text on his phone alerting him of the location change. The text had come in an hour before he'd seen it, so he'd had to make a beeline through traffic to get out to Brooklyn.

"Why the fuck would they move the meeting here?" Fresh asked as they neared the construction site.

"It's above your pay grade to ask that question," Judah said. "Somebody tells you to show up somewhere, you show up." He was walking a few paces ahead, anxious to get to the meeting.

"Even if we got no clue what we're walking into?" Fresh stopped in his tracks.

Judah stopped too, and glared back at Fresh.

"Judah, I don't mean no disrespect, but this shit feels janky. Think about it: all this backstabbing going on in the streets and now all of a sudden the meeting spot gets changed on us at the last minute?" Fresh shook his head. "All I keep thinking about is how they did Nicki Santoro in *Casino*."

"Fuck is you even talking about?" Judah started walking again.

Fresh wanted to elaborate, but what was the point? "Nothing, man." He let it go and fell in step with Judah.

For the first time since he had taken Fresh under his wing, Judah was starting to have second thoughts. Fresh was a solid young dude, a good earner, a natural leader of men, and his money never came up short. He soaked up information like a sponge, which made it easy for Judah to mold and teach him. Indeed, it was his ability to catch on quicker than most that had already earned him his own corner to hustle on. Fresh was turning out to be everything that Judah had hoped Cheese would be: a strong right arm. His only problem was that he was too damn inquisitive, always wanting to know why and how shit worked. Judah had initially thought that the kid's curious nature was a real strength. Unlike Cheese, Fresh was a thinker. Ever since he had questioned Judah about Ghost's murder, he'd been noticeably more rigid. Once, when Judah had reached out to change the radio station in the car, he could've sworn Fresh's hand inched closer to his gun. There was no doubt that the young boy knew more than he was letting on, and now the question was: what would he do with the information?

As they crossed the street, Fresh noticed a handful of soldiers hovering around the entrance of the construction site. He had never been to a meeting of this magnitude, and had expected to find a small army of soldiers there to protect their respective bosses instead of just this small gathering. There were two Latino kids he had never seen before and a young white dude wearing what looked like a top hat; Fresh would later learn that it was a shtreimel, a head covering sometimes worn by Hasidic Jewish men. He spotted two Black soldiers who he recognized as King associates.

One dude stood out more to Fresh even more than the man wearing the shtreimel. He didn't look much different than the scores of other hustlers Fresh had met in his young life—crisp button-down shirt, jeans, and Timberlands—but hanging from his neck was a metal pentagram. Fresh wasn't sure if it was because the guy was wearing sunglasses at night, or because the other soldiers seemed to be keeping their distance, but something just felt off. Fresh reasoned that the guy had to be connected to someone important, same as the rest of them.

Lil Man broke off from the group and moved toward Judah and Fresh when he saw them coming. He looked like an angry little bulldog sucking on a Newport. "You know you're late, right?" he said to Judah.

"Long story, but I'm here, ain't I?" Judah replied.

"Who this nigga?" Lil Man looked past Judah at Fresh.

"You know Fresh. That's my little man, Kev's baby brother."

Lil Man gave Fresh a once-over. "'Sup?" He nodded, then turned back to Judah. "Where your boy Cheese?"

"Taking care of something. We gonna stand here playing twenty questions or go handle this business?" Lil Man may have grown close to Monster over the past couple of months, but Judah was still Monster's second-in-command.

"You must ain't got the word," Lil Man said. "This meeting is for big boys only, so that means you're out here on guard duty with the rest of us."

"Fuck outta here!" Judah barked. "Me and Monster set this play up. Ain't no nigga in this clique got the rank or the right to tell me I'm sitting this out."

"Nobody except *him*." Lil Man motioned behind Judah.

Judah looked over his shoulder to see the truck carrying the King party pulling up to the curb. Monster came out first, followed by Chapman King and, to his surprise, Dickey Salvatore. Monster approached the soldiers and nodded in greeting, but it was Lil Man he embraced.

"Mostly everybody is here already," Lil Man told Monster. "I took the liberty of getting them settled until y'all got here. Ol' Hollywood," he gestured toward the man, "was the only one who insisted on waiting till the king arrived."

Monster spared a glance at the man, who didn't move or speak. "Everybody know where they're supposed to be?" Monster asked Lil Man.

"Yeah, or folks know the lick. These Spanish niggas seem glued to this main entrance, so we're gonna spread the rest of our people out. We just wanted to wait till you all got here and took your places so we'd know the best angles to keep eyes on you at all times."

"Solid." Monster pounded Lil Man's fist.

Chapman took stock of the men who had been assembled to provide security for the meeting. He gave a slight nod of approval before turning to the stranger with the dark glasses. "Tyriq Kane, the legend himself," he said, and shook the man's hand. "I'm glad you could make it."

"Who am I to refuse when the king requests an audience?" The man's voice was soft, but his words held power.

"I hope that at the end of this meeting, you'll find yourself persuaded to join our cause," Chapman said.

"Me and mine don't play well with others," Tyriq responded with a shrug. "The only thing I can promise is to keep an open mind."

"Fair enough." In truth, Chapman needed Tyriq and his people behind him more than anyone else. Though they were few in number, they possessed a certain skill set that had not been seen since the days of the Reapers. Having them on his side would all but guarantee that he'd come out of this war on the winning side. All the bosses of the underworld would be forced to kneel to the one true king—including Shai Clark.

"Where's your boy?" Monster asked. "What do they call him, the Mutt or some shit like that?"

"You mean the Hound?" Tyriq said. "He's around, same as always. Far enough not to hear anything that ain't for him, but close enough to kill every man here if this don't smell right."

"That some kind of threat?" Monster countered.

"Not at all. I was just answering your question. Or maybe you'd rather I called the Hound here so the two of you can have a sidebar conversation?" Tyriq smiled behind his dark glasses.

"I don't think that will be necessary," Chapman interjected. "My nephew was only busting your balls." He flashed Monster a dirty look. It wasn't smart to antagonize a man like

Tyriq Kane, and even dumber to provoke an audience with a serial killer. The Hound was little more than a myth to those too young to remember the grip of fear he'd held over the city back when he was still active. He'd been a real-life Candyman. The smart ones knew better than to even whisper his name in the darkest of corners. The stupid ones didn't believe that the stove was hot until they got their hands burned. Chapman had too much at stake to let his nephew fuck this up trying to prove he had the biggest swinging dick on the block. "Shall we go handle business?"

"After you, Your Highness." Tyriq gave an exaggerated bow and motioned for Chapman to lead the way.

Chapman entered one of the partially built structures first, with Dickey and Tyriq on his heels.

Monster stayed back to give some last-minute instructions to the soldiers. "Y'all make sure you keep your eyes open and hammers ready. Anybody or anything looks suspect, shoot it, ya heard?" He didn't wait for a reply before moving toward the building. When he noticed Judah at his side, he stopped. "'Sup?"

"Nothing. We rolling into the meeting, right?"

"Nah, I need you to hang back and keep these niggas on their toes."

"But I thought this was *our* thing."

"It is, and it will still be after the meeting is concluded." Monster started walking again.

Judah couldn't hide his anger and embarrassment. He'd been preparing for this moment ever since he'd double-crossed Ghost—the only dude who had ever tried to put him in position—and hitched his wagon to Chapman. Monster had promised him that when the time came and glory was handed out, Judah would be standing there to receive his. What was supposed to be his welcome to the inner circle had turned out to be a lesson about loyalty.

"Like I told you, nigga, you out here with us," Lil Man spoke up.

Judah wanted to pull his gun and empty the clip into the smug bulldog's face, but instead he rasped, "Fuck you!" and stormed off.

CHAPTER 21

All Dickey could do was laugh quietly to himself once they entered the construction site and peeped the setup. Whatever the Clarks had planned to build there was still in its infancy. Concrete had been laid, but only in certain areas. Everywhere else you had to walk over raw earth. The initial framework for the buildings had gone up, though not much else. There were pallets scattered around holding building supplies and bags of cement. They were standing in the middle of something that was to come, but hadn't quite arrived yet. It made perfect sense that someone as paranoid as Chapman King would choose to meet there. The open space left them exposed to the casual passerby or cop, but lacking walls to obstruct the view of the entire landscape meant there was nowhere for potential assassins to hide. It was fucking genius.

The business was to be discussed in the center of the site at a large picnic table surrounded by building materials. Already sitting at the table was Paul Schulman, a handsome fella with a head full of slick black hair, striking blue eyes, and a five-o'clock shadow lining his square jaw. He looked more like a movie star than a gangster. Sitting across from him was Orlando Zaza, an older Cuban man who was out of Miami but ran a successful franchise of cell phone stores in New York, Jersey, and Florida. He made good money from the stores, but his real business was guns. Standing near the head of the table, looking as nervous as a hooker in church, was the wild card: Mike Porter. Each of these men had played a key role in the betrayal and eventual ousting of Chancellor King. A traitorous bunch, the lot of them, who all had personal agendas. This made them the perfect candidates to replace the Monarchy's current Council of Lords.

"Welcome, friends," Chapman began once everyone else had taken a seat at the picnic table. "I'd like to thank you all for taking time out of your busy schedules to attend what I foresee to be a game-changing meeting. This day will usher in a better tomorrow for us all—"

"As you've been promising for the last few months," Paul Schulman jumped in. "But so far, all I see is open warfare in the streets. Blood is bad for business, which is something I believe we can all agree on." He looked around at the assembled faces.

"I'd have thought you of all people could appreciate the streets running red, Paul," Monster responded. "Wasn't it the blood of the lamb smeared on the doors of your ancestors that saved you from God's wrath?"

"Monster, that isn't called for," Chapman said, trying to keep the meeting on track.

"Neither is this sand-nigga coming in here trying to pass judgment about us doing what we gotta do to put things in order," Monster said. "Easy for him to sit back and point fingers, because ain't none of that blood made it to his door yet. Maybe that would change if word got out that he was the one who put that bullshit murder on my uncle." He had never cared for

Paul, and cared for him even less when he discovered the role he had played in dethroning his uncle.

They were all guilty of coconspiracy, this was true. But Paul's level of conniving trumped everyone else sitting there, with the possible exception of Monster. Monster might've turned a blind eye to his cousin's murder, which crippled a family already on the ropes, but it was Paul who'd made the move that landed the patriarch in prison. Chancellor had come to Paul with an offer to make an indictment hanging over his head disappear. In exchange, Paul was to clean up a situation involving one of Orlando Zaza's rivals. They'd each held up their end of the bargain, though Paul had changed the terms of the arrangement when he made an anonymous tip to the police, pointing them in Chancellor's direction.

Orlando shook his head. "Chapman, I gotta admit, when you promised you could get Chance out of the way, the snitch angle was something I didn't see coming. Never did I think I'd be sitting across a table from the rat and asked to break bread with him."

"Watch your mouth, Zaza," Paul said. "I'm no rat. I'm a businessman, same as everyone else sitting here. My hands are no dirtier than any of yours. Who here is without sin in this?"

"And your uncle was okay with this?" Mike asked Paul. He knew Benjamin Levitz from past dealings with his father, Alderman Porter. Benjamin was old-school, and working with a snitch wasn't his style.

"I don't have to report my every move to my uncle," Paul said.

"That's not even the punch line," Monster picked up. "Paul didn't frame my uncle for asking him to whack the guy who was giving you trouble, Mr. Zaza. He tied him up in a murder that my uncle had nothing to do with." He peered directly at Mike, who stared daggers right back at him.

"Wait," said Orlando. "You're telling me that Mike's the one who killed Alderman Porter? And if that's the case, why blame it on Chance?"

"I didn't have shit to do with what happened to Chance," Mike said. "I was raised under the G code, where we take out our enemies with pistols, not police." He was speaking to Orlando, but they all knew where the jab was directed. Mike's decision to kill his father had nothing to do with Chancellor King, though Chapman had found a way to bend things in that direction. Mike had been livid when he found out, but by then he was already in too deep to turn back. "And to answer your first question, it's a long story. But it's the same reason you smiled in Chance's face while plotting to put a knife in his back: you wanted something he had, and that was the quickest way to get it."

"In another life, this kid might've been one of us," Tyriq Kane said with a chuckle.

"None of that is important right now," Chapman interjected. "Most of us here had our own reasons for wanting my brother out of the way. Now that he is, let's move on from the past and discuss our futures."

It had only been twenty minutes since Monster led the group into the construction site for their meeting, and Fresh was already bored out of his mind. The two Cuban dudes who had come with Orlando chatted among themselves in Spanish. They wanted no interaction with the Black soldiers, and the feelings were mutual. Lil Man and the guys who had come on behalf of the Kings talked shit almost constantly. Lil Man kept going on and on about the plans he had for when Chapman finally made his move and the sour old men who were still running things were moved out of the way. Fresh didn't have to be a rocket scientist to grasp what he was talking about.

"Gotta take a leak," Fresh excused himself. The longer he listened to Lil Man speak, the more disgusted he became.

Judah still hadn't returned. He was probably licking his wounds. He had been running around like he was a big man on the streets, but Monster had shown him just how small he really was, dismissing him like he was little more than a corner boy. Served Judah right, as far as Fresh was concerned. Maybe now he knew how it felt to bust your ass for someone, only to have them treat you like you'd never spilled blood for them.

Fresh had been feeling some type of way about Judah ever since Judah and Millie had exchanged words. And some of the blanks were starting to get filled in. Thanks to Lil Man's chatty ass, Fresh now knew that Chapman was planning to use the men he was meeting with to move against the Monarchy. The same Monarchy that had just elevated him to power only a few months earlier. Fresh was a smart kid, but he felt like an idiot for having missed the signs: Ghost being killed and Monster sliding into his spot and promoting an outsider, Judah, to his number two instead of one of the generals who'd been a part of Ghost's inner circle. It had all been a part of one big plot— with Fresh now caught in the middle. Finding out that Judah was a world-class sucker had hurt, but it was nothing compared to what he felt knowing that he'd been riding with the men responsible for destroying his best friend's family.

Fresh had to make this right. But how? He had no idea.

He moved behind a tree to relieve himself. From where he was standing, he had a clear view of Chapman and the others. It looked like the discussion was getting heated; if Fresh was lucky, maybe they'd all draw their guns and murder each other. He laughed at the thought as he pulled his zipper up. He started to head back toward the others when something familiar touched the back of his head.

"'Sup, Fresh?" Shadow greeted his best friend with Lolli's P89.

"Fuck is you doing, Shadow?"

"I'm the one asking the muthafucking questions." Shadow pressed the gun harder against Fresh's skull. "Were you there? Did you stand with them when they killed my brother?"

"C'mon, Shadow. This is me . . . you know better than that."

"I only know what I see, and that's my best friend standing in the presence of my enemies. How could you, Fresh? Why would you do me like that?"

"Shadow, I had no idea Monster and Judah were involved until Millie went off on them earlier. The rest of it I only just pieced together."

Shadow grabbed Fresh by the front of his shirt with one hand and shook him, gun still to the side of his head. "You're a fucking liar and a traitor, same as the rest of them. And y'all are gonna see what you got coming!"

"After everything your family has done for me, you think I'd cross them?" Tears welled in Fresh's eyes. "I'd die for the Kings before I ever got down with something that would put you or your people in harm's way, and that's on my baby sister. One thing we ain't never do was lie to each other, Shadow. If in your heart you really think I could do something like that to you," he grabbed the barrel of Shadow's gun and moved it to the center of his forehead, "pull the trigger. End me right here and now, but it ain't gonna change my story . . . I didn't know."

Shadow looked deep into his best friend's eyes. He saw images of the two of them when they were kids playing in the schoolyard. He saw Fresh's mother giving him second helpings of her famous fried chicken. His finger tightened on the trigger. He tried to will himself to pull it . . . to splatter Fresh on the sidewalk like Judah had done to Ghost—but he just couldn't. He lowered the gun.

"Shadow—"

"Don't speak, Fresh. I don't wanna hear nothing out of your mouth. Just because I'm letting you live changes nothing between us. I can't fuck with you, dawg. You might not be a sucker, but you condone sucker shit, which is just as bad," Shadow fumed, echoing what Millie had said earlier. He started toward the construction site.

"What are you about to do?" Fresh called out.

"What the fuck does it look like? My family has been wronged and I'm the only one who can make this right."

"Only thing you're gonna do is get yourself killed if you try and roll in there on some John Wick shit. They got guys posted up at the other end of the site who'll be on your ass before you can fire a second shot."

"Fuck else am I supposed to do? I gotta go in there, Fresh!"

"Of course you do, but not without a plan."

CHAPTER 22

"So, what do you think?" Chapman looked around at the faces of the assembled to see how they would react to what he had just proposed.

"I think you are far more devious than any of us have ever given you credit for," Orlando said. "What your brother was offering would've made me a lot of money, but I see far more value in what you're bringing to the table. Who would say no to becoming a king?"

"Of your respective territory," Chapman reiterated. "The current Monarchy is comprised of small-minded individuals who are content controlling a single city. I want *all* of them! New York, Chicago, Miami, Detroit . . . We can spread across this country like wildfire, with each of you running your own kingdom. Of course, I'll still be the one true king, but whatever you do in the lands assigned to you will be your own business, so long as I get my taste. I'm offering each of you a brighter future."

"You're ambitious, Chapman, I'll give you that," said Paul. "But taking down one boss is a lot easier than taking down five. The Monarchy isn't going to sit on its hands and accept this retirement package you're planning to offer them."

"They won't have a choice," Dickey spoke up. "This ain't the seventies and eighties where old-school mob rules kept those ancient fucks in power. These days, it's soldiers like me and Monster who are out here making things happen, while men like my father sip their coffee and play chess, reaping the benefits of our hard work and feeding us the scraps. Personally, I'm tired of it, and I'm not the only one who feels that way. We've already been in contact with some of the captains and generals who serve the lords, and these young guys are hungry. *We* can be the ones feeding them."

"This is going to happen," Chapman continued. "Whether you join with us or not, the old Monarchy is out. When they're removed from power, anyone who isn't with us will be considered an enemy of the new regime. No more straddling the fence."

"Since you put it that way," said Paul, "I guess I'm in."

"I've already told you how I feel. May as well get to polishing my crown now," Orlando said with a grin. "But let me play devil's advocate for a minute. Chance's real power came from the political connections. Connections that you clearly don't have, Chapman. How are we supposed to compensate for that?"

"This is where Mikey comes in," said Monster. "Now that his daddy is no longer with us, he'll be the new shining jewel of the Porter clan."

"Behind the strength of his father's legacy, plus a little push from my family's connections in the Jewish communities," added Paul, "it shouldn't be too hard for us to move Mike into the next available city office. Of course, he'll have to start at the bottom, but he'll still be our man on the inside."

"So you killed your father to take his spot?" said Tyriq Kane. "That's some real biblical shit."

"Who's to say this won't turn into a repeat of what happened with Chapman?" said Orlando. "It's not too hard to imagine one of ours falling victim to the allure of becoming a big-shot politician and forgetting where his true loyalties lie."

"I'm more interested in the gold than the glory," declared Mike.

"So as you can see, we've covered all our bases," declared Chapman. "The only thing we need now is commitments from everyone at this table to move forward."

All but one of the men nodded.

"Kane, are you with us or not?"

Tyriq steepled his fingers as if he was mulling the question. After a few moments he replied, "As enticing as this all sounds, I must respectfully decline."

"What are you, stupid?" Monster said. "We're offering you the chance to be a king."

"I was a king long before either of your uncles knew what it felt like to wear a crown." Tyriq didn't mean this as a slight, it was simply a statement of fact. "I've seen this movie before, during the Blood Wars of my folk, and these games of power never end well." He had lost a lot of good souls during the Blood Wars, including his own children. He wasn't going to subject his people to something like that again, especially for someone like Chapman King, a man without a shred of honor. If the guy could cross his own brother and nephew, Tyriq held no illusions about what the new king of Five Points was capable of trying with him. "I'm grateful that you all even considered me to be a part of this, but I'm afraid my answer is still no. Now, if you'll excuse me . . ." He stood up from the picnic table.

"You know, it can get real cold out there when you're all by yourself in the world," said Orlando.

Tyriq smiled. "This won't be the first war of kings me and

mine have survived. Only the first that we are smart enough not to get involved in. You gentlemen have a good day." He promptly disappeared into the shadows of one of the structures being built.

"Fuck him!" Monster spat once he was sure Tyriq was out of earshot. "When we get this thing going, he and his whole fucking band of weirdo gypsies will be the first ones we wipe from the map. Ain't that right, Unc?"

"Shut up, Monster!" Chapman responded, more aggressively than he had intended. He'd been counting on the support of Tyriq Kane and his Gehenna assassins to tip the scales in his favor once the bloodshed began. Tyriq walking away from the table was something he hadn't accounted for—because of this, Chapman would have to pivot. Fortunately, he was good at making shit up as he went along.

For the next few minutes, the assembled members of what would become the new Monarchy listened as Chapman and Monster went over what would need to be done in the coming days and weeks. Even without the Gehenna, they still stood a pretty good chance of pulling it off. Everyone had an opinion, and no one seemed to mind talking over one another, so the chatter was almost deafening. Just beneath it, however, Chapman heard something.

"Everyone be quiet!" he shouted. He cocked his head, trying to zero in on the sound. It seemed to be a crunch of gravel coming from somewhere within the recesses of one of the structures. Someone was approaching.

"Who the fuck is that?" Monster raised his gun and aimed it in the direction of the sound. He strained his eyes and spotted Fresh emerging from the shadows. He wasn't alone. "The hell is this?"

"Damn, cuz, how come you don't look happy to see me?"

Shadow spoke from behind Fresh. He was holding his friend in front of him like a shield, and had a gun pointed at the side of his head. He ushered Fresh forward.

"Nephew, what exactly is it you think you're doing here?" Chapman called out.

"Righting a wrong," Shadow seethed. "And you lost the right to call me *nephew* when you crossed this family."

"Lil Cuz, I don't know if you're drunk or high on pills," said Monster, his gun still pointed toward Fresh and Shadow, "but I'm gonna need you to put that hammer down before you force me to do something we might both regret."

"You mean like when you turned a blind eye while that bitch-ass nigga Judah smoked my big brother?"

"Shadow, I don't know who you've been taking to, but they're pumping your head full of bad information. Put that gun down and let me talk to you real quick." Monster took a step forward, but jumped back when Shadow fired a bullet just short of his feet.

"Next one is in your dome, nigga. Back the fuck up!"

Monster complied.

"How could you, Monster?" Shadow continued. "From Chapman, we expected this kind of bullshit, but never from you. Ghost loved you like a brother, and you paid him back by letting him die!"

"Cuz, there are forces at work here that are bigger than both of us. Just chill." Monster knew the situation was about to take a turn for the worse, and he didn't want that for Shadow. Regardless of what had happened between he and Ghost, he still had love for his misguided little cousin.

"Really? What's bigger than family?" Shadow asked. "*All for the family*—remember that?"

Monster had no answer.

Shadow's gunshot had caught the attention of the soldiers posted up outside the site. They swarmed in, guns drawn, with Lil Man leading the charge. It only took a second for him to register what was going on: an enemy had breached the perimeter. The fact that it was Shadow King meant a trophy upon his fall. Lil Man didn't ask questions. He raised his gun and prepared to blast Fresh and Shadow both, but Monster stepped in the way.

"Hold your fire, Lil Man," said Monster. "He out of bounds, but that's still my little cousin. Shadow, you got balls. You've proven that by coming in here like this. But I need you to think this shit through. I'm trying to keep these boys off your ass, and your little shield don't hold as much value as you think. Fresh is a worker and easily replaceable. We can bust his brain to get to you, and I promise no one will lose any sleep over it. My ace trumps your king."

"Then how about a joker?" Pain appeared from behind one of the cement columns holding a rifle that looked like it had seen better days. The barrel was aimed at Chapman. "Fresh's passing might not mean nothing to y'all, but I can only imagine how far out of whack it would throw your little plans if I knocked the king's crown off."

"I see you got my message," Shadow called over to his friend. Pain's arrival had been a huge relief because he was more skilled at this kind of situation than Shadow or Fresh. Pain had been the very first person Shadow reached out to when he got it in his mind to break up this war party, but he hadn't been able to get in touch with him, so he'd gone at it alone.

"Indeed I did," Pain said. "Remind me later to get on your ass about how ignorant it was to leave a murder plot on my voice mail. Now," he addressed the group, "what I'm gonna need from the rest of you is to come up off them pistols I'm sure you're holding and toss them out of reach. Do it real slow too, so I don't get the idea that you're trying to be cute and put ol' Unc here to sleep."

"You shitting me?" one of the King soldiers challenged. "That *Little House on the Prairie*-ass gun is so old it probably don't even work."

In response, Pain shifted his rifle and pulled the trigger. The soldier's head burst, spraying blood in every direction. "Seems like it works pretty good to me. Anybody else want a test drive?"

The rest of the men wisely tossed their guns.

"This is going to go bad for you," said Chapman. "Even if you shoot me, there's no way you'll make it out of here alive."

"Me dying today is a strong possibility," said Pain, "but it's a gamble I take every time I step out of my house. Now, if you're done bumping your gums, let me tell you how the rest of this is going to play out. You and your boys—"

His words were cut off by another gunshot. Pain's eyes went wide and the rifle dropped from his hands. He slowly turned to find Judah standing behind him, holding a smoking pistol. "Sneaky muthafucka . . ." Pain croaked, before falling face-first to the ground.

"Guess y'all needed me at this little meeting after all, huh?" Judah sneered.

"Pain!" Shadow cried out.

"I tried to warn him." Chapman shook his head, looking down at Pain, who was coughing up blood.

Shadow felt like he was in a dream as he watched his friend bleeding out. Fresh was whispering something to him, but he couldn't hear it. He couldn't hear *anything*, in fact, other than his own heart thudding in his ears. The soldiers had already reclaimed their guns, which were all trained on him. Shadow realized he was going to die. Fresh too, and it would be his fault. If only he had listened to Millie and Lolli and let someone more qualified deal with the situation. His eyes turned to Chapman, who was looking at him with a smug expression on his face, and he could hear his mother's voice: *Do what needs to be done for this family.*

Shadow shoved Fresh aside and aimed his gun at Chapman. If he was going to meet his maker, the least he could do was bring his traitorous uncle along for the ride. "Die!" he screamed, then pulled the trigger.

Shadow would later replay this part of the night over and over in his head—he saw himself spitting some movie shit before airing out the enemies of his family. In reality, he'd held the gun loosely and off to the side, like gangsters in the movies he'd watched with Fresh and Pain. What they don't show you in those movies is how to compensate for the recoil. The bullet he had telegraphed to Monster's skull flew to the right and didn't even come close to hitting its target.

Shadow had shot his shot and missed the basket. Before he could fully process how bad he had fucked up, one of Monster's massive hands was already snatching the gun from him. As an afterthought, Monster slapped Shadow across the face. It wasn't hard enough to cause any real damage, but there was just enough force to steal whatever fire had been left in his little cousin.

"First rule of murder is: compensate for the kickback so you don't miss," Monster explained before shooting Shadow in the leg.

Chapman approached and peered down at Shadow, who had collapsed to the ground. "My poor, foolish nephew. Your daddy always warned you that you weren't cut out for this.

Maybe you should've listened to him instead of your mother, who I'm sure put you up to this. You ain't got the nuts to come up with something like this on your own."

"Fuck you!" Shadow clawed at Chapman, but his uncle sidestepped and kicked him in the face.

"You inherited your daddy's fierce will, I'll give you that. But that's about all." Chapman kneeled down so that he and Shadow were face-to-face. "The question is: do I kill you now, or let you live long enough to watch your mother and sister die? I'd planned on letting them live and die in poverty, but this little stunt you pulled tells me that the mercies I've shown this family have gone unappreciated."

"That's enough, Chapman," Mike stepped in. "The boy is no longer a threat. Let it be."

"Just because you're fucking my niece doesn't give you any say in what happens in this family," Chapman replied, to Mike's obvious surprise. "What, you didn't think I knew your little secret? My brother might've walked around with blinders on, but *I* see everything."

"I'll bet you didn't see this," Shadow rasped.

When Chapman turned back to his nephew, he saw a hand flash across his face. He stumbled back. At first he thought Shadow had punched up, but then he saw the bloody knife in the young man's hand. A moment later, he felt the hot burn of the slash Shadow had gifted him, cutting a line from the right side of his cheek up to his forehead.

"My face! You cut my face!"

"You're lucky—I was aiming for your throat," Shadow moaned.

"Kill that little bastard!" Chapman commanded, with his hands covering his bloody face. "But do it slow. I want him to suffer before he dies."

"Say less." Lil Man advanced with the remaining King soldiers in tow.

Shadow scooted backward, swinging the knife wildly to keep the men off him. He was in more pain than he'd ever experienced in his life, though fear and an overwhelming need to live kept him in the fight.

Lil Man circled around and managed to kick the knife out of his hand. Once Shadow was disarmed, they swarmed him, raining boots and fists.

Shadow tried to protect himself as best he could with only one good leg and one good arm. They stomped all over his body, landing a few good blows to his head. The fight had fled Shadow and he was just waiting for it all to end. His last thought was that long after he was gone, Chapman would be reminded of him every time he looked in the mirror.

Then came the darkness.

CHAPTER 23

Fresh watched helplessly as Lil Man and the goons beat Shadow to death. Tears flowed freely down his face and he felt like a coward, but he knew that if he tried to intervene, he would die right alongside his best friend. To his left he glimpsed Judah receiving a pat on the back from Monster. The scumbag was being treated like a hero. He had shot Pain in the back instead of facing him head-up. Fresh had stood on the sideline for far too long, and maybe if he had done something sooner, this wouldn't have happened.

He decided to act. He drew his gun and started inching his way closer to Judah and Monster. He had made it to within striking distance when something heavy fell from the sky and landed right in front of him.

"What the fuck?" Paul yelped as blood splattered his clothes. Something wrapped in a stained carpet lay on the ground right nearby. Everyone had guns drawn, scanning the tops of the building frames, trying to figure out where the rug had come from.

"Open it," Monster said to Judah.

"Why the fuck do *I* have to open it?" Judah asked.

"Because I told you to."

Mumbling under his breath, Judah peeled back the folds of the carpet. What he found inside almost made him vomit. Monster and the others gathered around to see what could make a man as tough as Judah turn as white as a ghost.

There was a beaten and bloodied body inside. But not just any body. This was Cheese . . . or what was left of him. His eyes had been plucked from their sockets and his lips were stitched closed. Carved into his chest were the words, *Suck my pretty dick!*

This was plainly Christian's response to Monster's decree.

Monster managed to tackle Chapman out of the way right as the first bullet struck. It sounded like the soft chirp of a bird, but left a golf ball–sized hole in Paul Schulman's head.

"Sniper!" Monster shouted, covering Chapman's body with his own.

The gathered soldiers all scrambled around, guns pointed skyward. Then came another chirp. This bullet struck one of Orlando's soldiers in the chest, sending him flying over the picnic table. Everyone scattered for cover.

From the shadows around several of the adjacent structures emerged a cluster of armed men, all dressed in black and carrying heavy firepower. Leading them was Christian, flanked by Jessie. Christian was wearing a black one-piece latex catsuit, and had a black bandanna tied gangster-style over his processed hear. Cradled in his arms was a golden AK-47. "I heard you boys were looking for me. Well, here the fuck I am!"

"You're dead, you fucking pansy!" Chapman shouted from under Monster's bulk.

Christian laughed. "If that ain't the pot calling the kettle black, with all the dicks that have blessed your soup coolers. I didn't come here to talk. I've come to return that crown you've been sporting to its rightful owner." He turned to his men. "Time to clean house, boys. Anybody who ain't one of us dies."

Chapman covered his ears against the deafening gunfire. He wasn't sure how many men Christian had with him, but it may as well have been over a hundred for the amount of bullets that were flying. This was going bad very fast. "Let me up," he said to his nephew, "I've got to do something."

"No chance, Unc. You're too important in all this for me to let you be killed before I get what you promised me. I've got to get you out of here." Monster pulled Chapman to his feet and moved in front of him as they tried to make their exit. One of Christian's men cut off their path and was rewarded by Monster with a bullet to the face. No sooner than he'd hit the ground, two more men appeared in his place.

"Where are they all coming from?" Chapman asked.

"Fuck if I know, but I can tell you where they're going." Monster fired another shot and looked around for Dickey, but there was no sign of him. This was typical. Dickey had always been good at leaving other people to clean up messes he had helped create. Monster would deal with the chicken later, but right then he needed to get Chapman to safety. He spotted Orlando to his left—the old man was holding his own, firing at enemies with the small gun he carried.

From out of nowhere appeared one of the biggest men Monster had ever seen. The guy moved toward Orlando with a speed that should've been impossible. What happened next, Monster would remember for the rest of his days, however long or short they may be.

Unlike his comrades, who were all carrying heavy weapons, the huge man didn't have a gun. At least not that Monster could see. Orlando hit him with two bullets to the chest at point-blank range, but he might as well have been shooting paper clips with a rubber band for all the effect they had. The big man knocked the gun away before wrapping one of his hands around Orlando's neck and lifting him off his feet. With his other hand, he grabbed one of Orlando's arms. The Cuban shrieked as the limb was torn from his body and discarded like a tree branch. The hulk dropped Orlando's body to the ground and set his sights on Monster and Chapman.

"Get out of here, Unc," whispered Monster. "I'll cover your exit."

"You're a braver soul than I gave you credit for, Nephew," Chapman whispered back as the predator marched toward them. "Dumb as a box of rocks, but brave."

"I might slap the shit out of you later for that, but right now I got a date with destiny." Monster rolled his powerful shoulders, preparing of battle. "If I fall here today, you make sure the streets remember my fucking name."

Monster and Frankenstein stood toe-to-toe, sizing each other up. Monster was a brute of a man, but Frank was built like a freak of nature. Monster had heard stories about Christian's pet giant and always wondered if he could take him. They glared at each other for several seconds.

Monster broke the silence: "So, you're the demon Christian keeps hidden under his bed, huh?"

"And you're the bitch who let the kin die who you were sworn to protect."

"I see that both our reputations precede us," Monster said.

"I didn't come here for your résumé, I've come for your head." Frank had known Ghost well and genuinely liked the man. He'd been looking forward to staring into Monster's eyes before tearing them out.

"Then come and get it." Monster tossed his gun aside.

* * *

Fresh was engulfed in chaos. Gunfire, coupled with screams of the dead and dying, filled the air. Christian had only rolled in with a handful of guys, but they'd swarmed Chapman's people like killer bees. If Fresh had heard someone else tell this story rather than being witness to it, he'd have called them a liar. There was no way something like this could happen outside of a movie, yet here Fresh was, trapped in the middle of it in real time.

He managed to dive under the picnic bench just as a bullet kicked up dirt and concrete in the spot where he'd been crouching. The cover of the wooden table allowed him a few precious seconds to breathe and take stock of the scene. He heard the familiar chirp again. This time he caught the muzzle flash and identified where it had come from. Perched in the frame of what would one day become a second-floor window was a dark-skinned dude with thick glasses, operating a sniper rifle mounted on a tripod. Fresh didn't know the guy personally, but had seen him once or twice and recognized him as Boogie, a member of Christian's traveling circus. Boogie moved the rifle left and right with a precision that could've only come from military training, plucking men off like tin ducks.

The sound of thunder now caught Fresh's attention. As far as he knew, there had been no rain in the forecast. Glancing around, he realized that it wasn't a storm, it was a clash of titans. Monster and Frankenstein were going at each other in the middle of all the gunfire. They stomped around, snarling like animals and raining blows powerful enough to break stones. It reminded Fresh of the *Godzilla vs. Kong* movie he had seen. To Monster's credit, he gave as good as he got, but the other giant's strength was on another level. Frankenstein managed to get Monster on his back, and straddled him before punching him repeatedly in his face. Fresh could feel the blows as if *he* was getting hit. He wasn't a religious man, but he prayed that Frankenstein would kill Monster.

Now Fresh heard a soft groan on the other side of the picnic table. Much to his surprise, the sound was coming from Pain, who was lying in a pool of blood, one hand outstretched with twitching fingers. His friend coughed blood into the gravel as he struggled to lift his face from the ground. To Fresh and Shadow, Pain had always seemed invincible, and the fact that he had been shot at close range and still had some fight left in him was a testament to his resilience. He managed to push himself to his knees, giving Fresh hope that he wouldn't lose two friends on the same day. But the hope evaporated when Judah and his gun appeared right behind Pain.

"You little niggas just don't know how to die, do you?" Judah shook his head.

Pain let out a forced laugh, blood spilling over his lips and down his shirt. "My teachers always said I was a poor student."

"Then allow me to give you a refresher course." As Judah looped his finger around the trigger, something struck him in the side and his shot flew over Pain's head. Then someone was on top of the Black Jew, trying to wrestle his gun away. Fresh wasn't surprised to see that it was Pain, and scrambled out from under the bench.

"I always knew you was a disloyal nigga," Judah spat in Fresh's direction as he hauled Pain off to the side.

"Nah, for once my loyalty is in exactly the right place," Fresh said before hitting him with a right cross.

Fresh could battle, but Judah was a gladiator. Fresh put up a good fight, yet he was no match. When it was over, Fresh was lying in the dirt with one of his eyes swollen closed and his chin feeling like it had been hit with a cast-iron skillet.

"We could've had it all, me and you." Judah hovered over him with his gun. "Were they worth it, Fresh? These same niggas who left you out in the cold when Malice was on your ass?"

Fresh looked from Shadow, who was unconscious, to Pain, whose blood was draining out of him. That was his clique: three the hard way since they'd been kids. There were no other men he would rather die with, so his answer to Judah was easy: "Absolutely."

The Black Jew shook his head. He really did like Fresh, and had he answered differently, he might've convinced himself to allow his protégé to live. "I should've let Malice have you," he said, and aimed the gun.

Fresh closed his eyes. He thought of his mother and sister, and the promise he had made to take them out of the ghetto. He conjured an image of himself, Shadow, Pain, and Voodoo at Jones Beach. It had been the first time he and Shadow had a fight. All because he had snatched off Voodoo's bikini top. Shadow had been pissed and would've likely cut Fresh with the broken bottle he chased him around with, had Pain not stepped in. No blood had been shed that day. Instead, they spent the night sharing a six-pack of Cisco and ended it by taking Pain to the hospital to be treated for alcohol poisoning. "Good times," he now said out loud to no one in particular.

Fresh heard a gun go off and braced himself for the impact that never came. He waited a few seconds before daring to open his eyes. Judah was lying on the ground in front of him, brains seeping out from a hole in the side of his head. Standing behind him was Mike Porter, his 9mm still raised. Fresh was too stunned to speak, so his mouth flapped open and closed like a beached fish.

The only explanation Mike offered before slipping away was a simple nod. Fresh didn't know what this meant, and didn't care. He was just thankful to be alive. And he had to get Pain and Shadow out of there before his luck turned.

Fresh picked himself off the ground and hobbled over to where Shadow had fallen. To his surprise, Shadow was gone. The only sign that his friend had been there at all was a trail of blood leading out of the construction site.

EPILOGUE

By the time Lolli arrived with Nefertiti to the address she'd been sent, the site was already crawling with police. Uniformed officers kept the gathering crowd of spectators at a distance, while detectives combed the crime scene for clues. At least seven body bags had been carried out and loaded into meat wagons. Someone had come through there on demon time, laying shit down. Who? Lolli still wasn't sure, but she had an idea. She prayed that none of those bags held her little brother. It would be several hours before Nefertiti could confer with some of her contacts in the police department and learn that Shadow King hadn't been among the corpses, though there was a Melvin King who had been taken into custody.

The police had found Monster unconscious at the construction site. Someone had fucked him up pretty badly. The way Lolli heard it, his worst injuries were a fractured cheekbone and a concussion. Monster was an unstoppable force, and Lolli had no idea who or what could've inflicted that kind of damage on him.

Monster had been rushed to the hospital and later taken into custody as a suspect in the multiple homicide. Lolli would've paid good money to be there when Monster woke up and found out that he had been placed under arrest. Had Lolli found him *before* the police, he would've been dead. Chapman would no doubt use his Monarchy connections to get Monster out on bond, but it would take awhile. For now, at least, he was out of the way and one less problem for Lolli to worry about.

She was surprised to find out that a kid named Percy Wells had also been taken to a hospital, having suffered a gunshot wound. That was Pain's government name. If he was alive, maybe Shadow was too. Lolli checked hospitals, morgues, and precincts, but none of them had any record of a man fitting Shadow's description having been brought in. It was impossible for him to have just up and vanished, so where the hell was he? As this question rattled around in Lolli's brain, she took solace in the fact that her baby brother hadn't been listed among the dead or locked up.

Lolli had Nefertiti drop her off at her mother's apartment. She was tired and wanted to go home, but figured that Maureen had already received word of what had happened and was worried sick over her baby boy. She let herself into the apartment and heard her mother speaking to someone in the kitchen. Lolli became hopeful, thinking it might be Shadow. Maybe he hadn't been at the massacre after all? She went into the kitchen to find a man sitting across the table from Maureen, but it wasn't her brother.

Lolli drew her gun and aimed it at her mother's guest. "Ho-ass nigga! You must've lost all your scruples to show up here after what you've done."

"Lauren, let me explain." Mike Porter stood, waving his hands in surrender. His clothes were dirty and torn, and his face looked like he had been in a fight.

"Explain it to God, because I don't wanna hear it."

Maureen jumped from her seat and moved between her daughter and Mike. "Lolli, put the gun down."

"Fuck that, he got to die, Ma!" Lolli stepped around her mother and closed in on Mike. She didn't give a shit what her mother thought, there was no one short of God who could save this man from her wrath. He was a traitor and would be dealt with accordingly.

"Lauren!" Maureen shouted in a tone that Lolli hadn't heard since she was a little girl and had gotten caught fighting with boys in the street. "You need to hear him out. Mike has something to tell you that might change everything."

When Mike finished speaking, Lolli felt like her head had been screwed on backward. She'd known there had been a major plot, but now she realized she had no clue just how deep the rabbit hole went. "And you believe this line of bullshit?" she asked Maureen.

"It makes sense to me," her mother answered, "and right now it's all we have to go on."

Lolli turned back to Mike. "I've gotta admit, you've filled in a lot of blanks tonight. But you still haven't answered the most important question."

"And what's that, Lauren?" Mike said.

"Where the fuck is my brother?"

Shadow awoke to devastating pain. His head throbbed like the worst hangover of his life, and his wrist felt like someone was jabbing a knife into it. He couldn't feel his leg that had been shot, and wondered if that was a good or a bad thing. Either way, he knew he was seriously fucked up.

Something cool was pressed against his head and it made the pain recede, but only a little. He could make out the silhouette of a woman at his bedside. "Ma?" he said, his throat dry and scratchy.

"No, but thank you for the compliment."

Shadow's vision began to clear. "Who the fuck are you?"

"The bitch who saved your life," replied Jessie, the trans woman. "I'd think you'd show a bit more gratitude."

"I'm sorry, I didn't mean it like that. *Where* am I?"

"Not the afterlife, that's for sure," Christian chimed in from the other side of the room. He was still wearing the latex catsuit, which was now shredded, though he'd abandoned the bandanna. His face was covered in bruises and blood splatter that he'd done a poor job of wiping away. "Jessie spotted you sleeping off that ass-whipping and suggested we get you out of the way, less you get stepped on again."

"What happened?" Shadow asked.

"Long story," Christian said, "but the short version is you almost got yourself killed, along with a few other poor souls in the process."

"Pain?" Shadow vaguely remembered seeing Judah gun his friend down.

"Alive, but he'll likely have to sit for a time until he can come up with a proper explanation for being at the scene of a multiple homicide. He should be the least of your concerns right now. Word on the streets is that the little facelift you gave your uncle didn't earn you any friends. Congratulations, you've been officially declared an enemy of the crown."

"Like I give a fuck! Chapman got no right to that crown anyhow. It should be—"

"Yours?" Christian cut Shadow off. "Little boy, you ain't no more fit to wear that headdress than your conniving-ass uncle. It takes a strong neck to hold that kind of weight, and frankly, you ain't quite up to it."

"And *you* are?" Shadow said.

"Heavens no." Christian held up his hands. "Last thing I need is some gaudy showpiece fucking up my hairdo." He patted his finger waves. "I have no desire to waste this beautiful life of mine looking over my shoulder. When I die, it's going to be between a set of beautiful legs, not in some fucking gutter with a hole in my head. Unlike Chapman, I have no aspirations for something that don't belong to me."

"This ain't about power," said Shadow, "it's about right of blood."

"I hear you. You ain't wrong, but you ain't quite ready either. The dumb shit you pulled at that construction site is proof of that. See, you got all the heart in the world, but what good is heart if you ain't got no smarts to go with it? Boy like you, all angry because he got his allowance cut off . . . ? Chapman and Monster should've seen you coming a mile away. You had the element of surprise on your side this time, but I doubt you'll be so lucky again. The reason you failed is because you wear your intentions on your sleeve. You gotta learn how to bury those impulses and project only what you *want* people to see. By the time they realize it's an illusion, it'll be too late."

"Are you talking about *The Art of War* or something?" Shadow asked.

"No, sweet Prince, I'm talking about the Masquerade."

TO BE CONTINUED . . .

THE RELUCTANT KING
BOOK ONE IN THE RELUCTANT KING SERIES

The King family is on the political rise in New York City, but must weather the violent storm wrought by their darkest secrets.

"K'wan is exceptionally gifted at ratcheting up suspense . . . There's no denying the writer's talent for dark, gritty fiction. It's a page-turner." —*Kirkus Reviews*

"New York City Council member Chancellor King and his socialite wife are regarded as modern-day royalty, but King's ambition to rise in the political world is threatened by an unambitious son and some dark family secrets." —*Publishers Weekly*

Also available by K'wan from Akashic Books

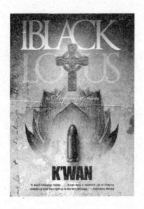

BLACK LOTUS

Finding the Black Lotus murderer is Detective Wolf's chance to avoid an Internal Affairs investigation. That's when things get personal.

• Selected for the Library Services for Youth in Custody 2015 In the Margins List
• One of *Library Journal*'s Best African American Fiction Books of 2014

"[A] heart-thumping thriller . . . K'wan does a masterful job of keeping readers on their toes right up to the very last page."
—*Publishers Weekly*

BLACK LOTUS II: THE VOW

After the death of a police officer, assassin Kahllah (aka the Black Lotus) is forced out of retirement in an attempt to clear her name while outrunning a mysterious enemy.

• Nominated for the 2021 Street Lit Writer of the Year Award, presented by the AAMBC Awards

"From page one to the last, *Black Lotus 2: The Vow* is a high-wire act with no net. A smart refiguring of hard-boiled with a nitro injection of new-age sensibilities." —Reed Farrel Coleman, *New York Times* best-selling author of *Sleepless City*